DRIVING
HER CRAZY

A CRAZY LOVE STORY

KIRA ARCHER

Entangled Publishing, LLC
2614 South Timberline Road
Suite 109
Fort Collins, CO 80525
Visit our website at www.entangledpublishing.com.

Lovestruck is an imprint of Entangled Publishing, LLC.

Edited by Erin Molta and Heather Howland
Cover design by Heather Howland
Cover art from iStock

Manufactured in the United States of America

First Edition August 2015

To the hubs and my kidlets. You are my world.

Chapter One

Honk! Honk!

Cherice Debusshere slowly blinked open her eyes and stretched. The sun filtered in through her half-drawn blinds, sending pale yellow stripes across her duvet—

Wait. The sun?

She grabbed her phone. 8:14 a.m.

"Crap!"

The alarm was definitely still set, but it hadn't gone off. She did a quick check.

"You've got to be kidding me," she groaned, jumping out of bed. She'd set the damn thing for six p.m., not six a.m. She ducked under her blinds and stuck her head out the window. The town-car idled at the curb. As if to rub it in, the driver honked again. Cherice groaned.

She was going to miss her plane.

Her mother was going to *kill* her.

Scrambling around her apartment she tossed shoes,

hairbrush, deodorant, and her favorite shampoo and face wash into her carry-on bag. She shoved her legs into a tasteful pair of slacks, tucking in the matching silk shell tank, and grabbed a delicate cashmere sweater to go over it. Her mother had always told her to dress her best, because you never know who you might meet, and as Cherice pulled out the few pieces of clothing that her mother would approve of *and* would make her feel good—she could mix and match for the weekend—she sighed and folded them carefully in her bag.

Her doorbell rang.

"Crap," she muttered again. Her foot got tangled in the strap of the purse she'd left on the floor and she hopped over to the door while trying to extricate it. She needed to slow down before she killed herself. But slowing down would make her more late. Late was bad.

She pulled the door open, her heart pounding like she'd run up five flights of stairs. The driver stood waiting, hands clasped in front of him.

"Hi, I'm Cherice," she said, holding out her hand.

He looked surprised but shook her hand. "I'm Tim."

"Nice to meet you. I'm almost ready."

He nodded. "Can I take your luggage?"

"Oh. It's not quite ready yet."

"Would you like me to wait?"

"No, that's all right, thank you. I'll bring it down."

"Yes, ma'am." He looked at his watch. "If we don't leave soon…"

"I know, I know. Sorry. I'll be right there."

He nodded again and headed back down the stairs.

Cherice hurried to the bathroom and brushed her teeth

in record time, grabbing a glass of water to rinse her mouth. A quick glance at the clock on the wall made her inhale and choke. It didn't *tick* so much as taunt. *Late, late, late, late, late.*

She tossed the remains of her water in the direction of Betty, the potted plant on her counter, and missed. She groaned. The poor thing was finally showing renewed signs of life. It would suck to lose her now.

Cherice made sure the little inverted water bottle was still propped up in the dirt, holes properly drilled so it would slowly leak water into the soil. She'd Googled ways to keep plants watered while on vacation. Hopefully, this worked.

"You hang in there, Betty," she murmured to the plant while softly stroking its leaves.

She wiped her mouth and then mopped up the mess on the counter. The water would dry just fine if she left it, but it would leave spots. It might be her personal bathroom, but that, as her mother would say, was no excuse to cut corners. She might fail at most of the life lessons her mother had taught her, but damn it, her apartment was always guest-ready and she always looked her best.

Tim honked again. She hung her head out the window and shouted down to him. "I'm coming!"

Luckily, her mom had the bridesmaid's dress she was wearing, so she didn't have to worry about that. Her suitcase was overstuffed, but she didn't have the time to pack it more carefully.

Cherice shoved a necklace and some bangles in her pocket, tossed her makeup bag in her purse, and ran out the door. It hadn't even closed yet before she shoved it back open, her anxiety ratcheting up another notch at the delay.

She snatched her suitcase and rushed out, locking the

door behind her. Thankfully, she'd checked in via her cell phone last night and had taken care of everything she needed to for her apartment the week before. She'd found someone to cover for her at the DressHer disadvantaged women's location where she spent most of her time, and her personal shopping clients were aware she was on vacation for a week. One of the perks of working for herself. Time off whenever she wanted.

As soon as the car took off, she pulled her makeup bag out of her purse. Some base powder and a little eyeshadow brightened her face a bit. Things were going okay until she went for the eyeliner.

The liner went on in a nice, even line. Until the car hit a pothole. Her hand jerked, leaving her with an inch-long black line shooting out from her eyelid.

"Sorry, ma'am," Tim said.

"That's okay."

It wasn't okay. But it wasn't his fault she'd decided to do her makeup in the car.

The theme song from "Game of Thrones" rang from her purse and Cherice sighed, the little ball of dread in her stomach growing bigger.

Her mother.

She fumbled her phone out of her purse.

"Hello?"

"Cherice. Are you at the airport?"

Cherice took a deep breath. She wasn't even in New York yet and she was already going to piss off her mother.

"I'm on my way."

A faint sigh echoed from the phone. "You should always leave yourself at least two hours to go through security."

"I know. I meant to but—"

"It doesn't matter. Just make sure you don't miss your flight. I hope the weather won't be an issue." Her mother sighed. "Of all the weekends to have a summer storm."

"Is it causing problems up there?"

"Not for me, so far. But with the reception outdoors, even with the tent, anything more than a light drizzle could be a disaster. I had to pull a lot of strings to get this wedding in the Times. I'll never live it down if it's not perfect."

"I'm sure it's going to be beautiful, Mom."

"Yes. Well. Just be sure you get here on time. The rehearsal dinner is this evening. You are part of the wedding party. Your absence will be noted."

Cherice winced, breathing past the guilt and hurt feelings that were a normal part of conversations with her mother. Her absence would be noted, not because they'd actually miss her but because she'd throw off the balance of the perfectly organized wedding party. Not that she blamed her mom for wanting everything to go off without a hitch. The vultures her mother called friends really would torture her with it for the rest of her life if anything went wrong.

"I'll be there."

"I hope so. Oh, the journalist who is writing the feature is here. I must run."

The phone clicked before she could say goodbye.

She dropped her phone back in her purse. Her mom was always short with her, but Cherice didn't think it was personal. The woman was just…supremely efficient…and insanely busy. Always. Especially with her sister's wedding a day away. But once in a while, it'd be nice if her mother would call her just to talk to her, not chastise her for some mistake she hadn't even made yet.

With a sigh, Cherice cleaned up her face. Thankfully, she managed to apply the rest of her makeup without any further complication. Her necklace and bracelets went on last. There. Perfectly presentable. Even her mother couldn't complain.

Her leg bounced all the way to the airport and it took a Herculean effort not to chew her nails to the quick. She'd blown off Thanksgiving, had just barely made Christmas (two days), and ditched New Year's entirely. She'd also pretended she was sick for Easter. If she missed her sister's wedding she'd be disowned. And that wasn't an exaggeration.

Cherice was already the black sheep without ruining what was supposed to be one of *the* social events of the year. She didn't have an important job, she wasn't in school anymore, since her abysmal MCATs had pretty much derailed her medical career, and she wasn't involved in some illustrious relationship. Therefore, she had no justifiable reason to mess up her mother's flawless plans.

"Are you okay, ma'am?" Tim asked.

Cherice made an effort to stop her leg from bouncing and smiled at him. "I'm fine, thanks. Going up to New York to visit my family and I'm just a little nervous."

"Afraid of flying?"

She laughed. "No. Afraid of my family."

He grinned at her in the rear view mirror. "They can't be that bad."

"You'd be surprised," she said. "My sister is getting married this weekend and my mother is in full meltdown mode."

He shook his head. "I sympathize. My oldest daughter was just married a few months ago. My wife was…" He laughed. "Let's just say I was very happy when the wedding was over."

"Good to know my family isn't the only one that goes crazy over weddings."

"It would be weird if they didn't."

The car pulled up outside the airport and Tim came around to unload her bag and open her door. Cherice had already paid for the car service, but she handed him a generous tip.

"Any advice for how to survive this weekend?"

Tim grinned. "Keep your head down, stay out of their way, do everything you're told to do quickly and without argument."

Cherice laughed. "I'll do my best."

"Don't worry. As soon as it's over they'll be back to normal."

"Ah, I was feeling better until you said that. Normal isn't really an improvement."

He tipped his hat to her. "Good luck, ma'am."

"Thanks."

She grabbed her things, gave Tim one last grateful smile, and ran. Well, she walked. Briskly. Running in public would create a scene and that wasn't something Debussheres did. Besides, she didn't want to find out how well her Jimmy Choos fared at high speeds on pockmarked sidewalks.

Cherice barreled into the building and headed straight for security, cell phone in hand and her ID ready, but pulled up short when she saw the winding line in front of her. Were there even enough people in her town, let alone flying out this morning, to create such a ridiculous line? She absolutely couldn't miss her flight. But as long as nothing else went wrong, she should be fine. She hoped.

Cherice sent up a quick prayer that for once in her life she'd get lucky.

Nathaniel Oserkowski threw a few pairs of jeans, a couple T-shirts, and the other basics into a suitcase. The only items he bothered folding were a pair of slacks and a nice, white polo shirt.

"Oz, you can't pack your stuff like that. Everything will get wrinkled."

His sister, Lena, took everything out and started to neatly fold and repack.

"The only things I care about getting wrinkled are my interview clothes and I folded those."

She rolled her eyes and kept packing, pausing only to tell her five-year-old son, Tyler, to quit jumping on the bed.

The little boy bounced onto his butt and propped his chin in his hands, his elbows resting on his knees.

"You going away, Uncle Oz?"

"Yep, but just for a few days. I'll be back before you even miss me."

"Promise?"

Oz's heartstrings tugged and he scooped his nephew up. "I promise." He kissed the top of his head and dropped him back to the bed.

"All right, you two," Lena said. "We've got to get Uncle Oz to the airport. You have everything?" she asked him.

"Yes."

"You sure?"

He sighed. He loved his sister but sometimes she acted way too much like his mother. "Yes, Lenny."

She chucked a pair of balled up socks at his head. "You're such an ass."

He grinned at her and zipped up his suitcase.

"You got someone to cover your paper route, right?" she asked.

"Yes. And before you ask, I'm using my vacation days for the garage and one of the other janitors at the university is going to cover for me this weekend."

Lena frowned. "Well, hopefully you'll be coming home with a brand new job and you can quit all the rest of them."

Ah man. From her lips to God's ears. When his sister had kicked her good-for-nothing boyfriend out, opting to raise their baby on her own rather than let the jerk stay in their lives, there hadn't been a question of what Oz would do. He'd found a small house, quit school, and worked as many jobs as he needed to keep the bills paid.

Sure, he had moments where he missed the kind of life he might have had, but he didn't regret his choice to take care of his family for a single second.

Lena chipped in when she could. When she'd moved in, they'd made the decision that she'd stay home with Tyler until he was in school full-time. She'd been trying for years to start some sort of business. Some with more success than others. A lot of her ideas tended to be too big in scale for her to pull off. Or just plain crazy to work. But, she did usually manage to bring in a couple hundred every month between her Etsy store and reselling things she found around town on eBay.

With Tyler getting ready to start kindergarten, Lena

had been looking for a "real" job. Tyler's school was looking for teacher aides, which would be perfect, since she'd be working the same hours he was in school. It didn't pay great, but it'd be enough that Oz could probably quit his weekend janitor job.

If he could land the desk editor job, though... He'd be able to quit everything else *and* give Lena and Tyler the life they deserved. It was something he'd be able to do from home, to boot. He wasn't sure what he'd do with all the spare time. All he knew was that it would be really, really nice not to have to spend every moment of every day working. He needed a break.

"Keep your fingers crossed," he said.

"And my toes."

"And my eyeballs!" Tyler chimed in.

"Thanks, buddy. I'm sure that will help."

Lena grabbed her purse. "All right, boys! Load up!"

It took forty-five minutes to get to the airport, and by the time they arrived, Oz was in need of a few aspirin and a good long nap. His nephew was the light of his life, but being trapped in a car with an amped-up five-year-old was enough to drive anyone to pharmaceutical intervention.

They parked in the short term lot and Oz raced Tyler to the entrance. Well, Tyler raced. Oz did his slow-mo runner routine. His and Lena's dad had always done that when they were kids. Challenge them to a race or an arm wrestle match or something and then pretend that his muscles had disappeared so he couldn't even hold up his arm or was stuck in molasses and could barely move his feet. Oz had always loved it. Tyler's real dad wasn't ever going to be in the picture but Oz tried his damndest to be the best father figure he could for his nephew.

Tyler "won," but just barely. They tumbled through the doors, laughing.

Until he saw the length of the security line.

Oz gave a low whistle. "I hope we got here early enough. Usually it doesn't take all that long."

"Uncle Oz!" Tyler said, tugging on his hand.

"What's up, little man?" he said, squatting down to Tyler's level.

"Look at the fancy lady. Is she the principal?"

Oz looked in the direction Tyler was pointing and chuckled. The principal of Tyler's new school always made it a point to welcome all the new incoming kindergarteners and she'd been dressed very nicely when she'd come to their home. Since Tyler spent a lot of time hanging out with Oz down at the shop, he was more used to seeing men and women in greasy coveralls than dressed up in business attire.

"No, she's not the principal."

"She's pretty," Tyler whispered.

Oz couldn't argue that. The woman was gorgeous. But she was also standing in line at the airport dressed like she was about to walk into some board meeting and she was digging around in a purse that looked like the one Lena had been lusting after for years. It was worth more than his first car.

"Yes, she is," Oz agreed, picking his nephew up again and giving him a big kiss. Tyler squealed with laughter and tried to squirm away but Oz kept a firm hold on him.

"Fly me, Uncle Oz!"

Oz laughed. "You're getting too big to be an airplane," he said, but he hefted him higher, anyway. He was going to miss the little rascal.

Lena frowned. "Do you want us to wait with you?"

Oz knew the tone of her voice. She didn't want to leave him alone, but the thought of keeping Tyler contained in a busy airport was enough to induce a panic attack in the strongest of mothers.

"No, you guys can go on home. It might take a while."

"Okay," she said, not bothering to hide her relief. "But you call the second you land."

"Yes, ma'am."

She mock glared at him and he laughed. "All right, Tyler," she said. "Give Uncle Oz a hug goodbye."

Oz said his goodbyes, hoping like hell he'd come home with good news. He was tired of working three jobs just to make sure ends did more than just barely meet. And if he could support everyone doing something he loved, life would be pretty damn good. The desk editor job was a long shot. But it was one he had to take.

Maybe he'd get lucky for once in his life.

Chapter Two

Cherice switched her carry-on to her other shoulder so she could dig in her Louis Vuitton for some lip gloss. The line was moving very, very slowly. With every step she shuffled forward, her concern doubled. If she didn't have high blood pressure by the time she got out of here it would be a miracle. Crap, crap, crap.

Every few minutes someone's deep, baritone laugh would ring out, rippling through Cherice in waves of warmth and good naturedness. Really, who was in that good a mood stuck in an interminable line at the airport? And could he please share whatever he was on, because she could use a healthy dose of it.

The sound of a child laughing drew her attention to a small family a few feet away. The father, a ridiculously handsome man who could have graced the cover of *GQ*…well, maybe *Popular Mechanics*, she amended, taking in his worn jeans and scuffed boots, was holding a curly-haired blond boy in the air above his head. The boy shrieked in delight, kicking his legs, while his mother looked on with a beaming smile.

The man snuggled the boy in his arms for a moment, giving him a loud kiss on the cheek before handing him back to his mother. She wrapped her free arm around the man's waist and hugged him, patting him on the chest with an encouraging expression. Pep talk? Maybe the guy was afraid of flying. Though Cherice didn't see how anyone with the rock hard biceps of a Greek god could be afraid of anything.

The man gathered his family in his arms, giving them a lingering hug, and for a brief moment Cherice wished she were the one wrapped in that embrace instead of the bubbly-looking little blonde he was holding. Cherice tore her gaze away from the tender family moment, almost squirming in shame for ogling a married man. No matter how drool-worthy he was.

Another security guard opened up a second line and things finally started moving. The chiseled and very unavailable hunk got into line a few people behind her and struck up a conversation with whoever was next to him. Friendly, wasn't he? Cherice looked down at her phone and sucked in a panicked breath. Her flight! She closed her eyes and sent up another quick prayer since the first one didn't seem to have worked. If she missed that flight, she was toast.

Finally, she was a few people back from the checkpoint. She slipped off her shoes, and juggled them with her phone and ID. As soon as she was close to the little trays on the conveyor belt she dumped everything in, pushing them as far ahead as she could get them. Maybe it would make the people in front of her hurry up. She was down to fifteen minutes until her flight departed.

She hefted her suitcase onto the conveyor and shoved it through the plastic square. Well, partly. Halfway through, the suitcase got wedged. Cherice shoved on the bag, trying to squish everything down so it would fit.

Finally, it popped through, nearly sucking Cherice in with it. Relief flooded her. Her mother always said to never check any luggage if you were flying commercial. You never know who could riffle through it on the way or if it would make it to your destination at all. Cherice shoved the rest of her belongings through the square and hurried through the metal detector, nearly swearing aloud when the damn thing beeped. A female guard pulled her to the side and asked her to empty all her pockets, while the people in line behind her sailed through without any problems.

"There's nothing in my pockets. It was probably just my jewelry," she said, removing the gold chain and bracelets. She'd give the damn things to her if the woman would just let her leave. "I didn't think it was enough metal to set the detector off."

"Sorry, ma'am, but we have to perform a search if the alarm is triggered."

"Is that really necessary? I'm going to miss my flight. I'm sure it was just my necklace."

"I'm sorry, ma'am. Just step over here please."

Cherice stood rigid while the woman wanded her. She was quick, methodical, and totally professional, but Cherice was late and getting more so, by the second.

As soon as it was determined that Cherice was not, in fact, smuggling a weapon of mass destruction in her lacy underwire, she marched back to the screening area to retrieve her suitcase and handbag. Where yet another job-conscious security guard in plastic gloves was standing over it like a guard dog.

"I'll need to search through your bag," he informed her.

"Is that necessary?"

"Yes, ma'am. Sorry. Do you have anything sharp or liquid in here?"

"No. Not really. Just some lotion I think."

He riffled through her bag, pulling out a few items as he went through it.

"I'm sorry, ma'am, but these items aren't allowed on board," the guard said, gesturing to a growing pile of her belongings.

It had to be some kind of weird conspiracy. "It's just some hand sanitizer and fingernail clippers. I assure you I have no intentions of using those for anything other than nail care," she said, trying for a playful smile. "Wait. Why isn't the lotion allowed?"

"I'm just doing my job, ma'am."

"I know, and I appreciate that. I don't mean to be a pain, but really? I can't very well moisturize anyone to death."

He ignored that remark. "Anything over three ounces isn't allowed. Any other liquid items should be stored in a clear plastic baggie. Do you have any items in your suitcase that might be a problem?"

She didn't want to answer that but they'd already scanned her suitcase and were opening it, so she nodded. "My shampoo and face wash. Some perfume."

He nodded and looked at his fellow guard who was already removing the items.

"Okay, the rest is fine."

Cherice focused on taking deep breaths and swallowing the snippy remarks that she couldn't help thinking. She was seconds from missing her flight and this had just gone beyond ridiculous. If she missed that plane, she'd never hear the end of it. Her parents had wanted her to come out a full week before her sister's wedding, but the prospect of facing that much time being constantly reminded of what a huge disappointment she was had been too much to consider. She'd insisted she was too busy and flying in the day before would be more than enough time.

Just the thought of hearing her mother's smug *I told you so* was enough to make her skin crawl. She wanted to scream but the poor man clumsily shoving her jewelry and belongings back in her bag wasn't at fault. She counted to five. Ten. It was her own damn fault she'd gotten there late and not checked the airline's website for the rules. She wasn't going to take her frustrations out on him.

He handed her phone back to her but in her haste to get moving again she grabbed for it too quickly, succeeding in knocking the thing from his hand. It landed neatly against the shoe of the man who'd just come through the metal detector.

The man from the sweet little family gathering she'd noticed before.

He bent down and picked it up, handing it to her with a smile that would have struck her speechless under normal circumstances. Who was she kidding? She couldn't wrestle up a coherent thought at that moment if he paid her to.

"I think you dropped this," he said, his deep voice sliding through her like warm honey. He grinned at her again. "Everything all right, miss?"

Well, my, my. Rhett Butler to the rescue.

The faint Southern accent that tinted his speech did interesting things to parts of her that had no business being charmed by a married man. But it was kind of hard to ignore. She'd always been a huge fan of southern gentlemen, part of the reason she'd picked North Carolina when making her escape from her mother's clutches.

She gave him a careful smile. Grateful, but not interested. She didn't want him to mistake gratitude for flirting. He exuded strength, good will, and all around happiness. And that was just wrong. How in the hell could anyone have stood in that line for the last hour and gone through the privacy invasion brigade and still be in a good mood? It was totally unfair. He was probably a morning person, too.

He *had* managed to distract her from her rapidly disintegrating mood, though. And the fact that he'd called her miss and not ma'am like she was some eighty-year-old biddy won him some serious brownie points.

Those sparkling blue eyes of his were still smiling into hers and she looked away. He handed the purse to her and led her away from the congested security area to where she could actually take a few deep breaths.

"I'm fine," she said. "As good as anyone can expect to be, I suppose, when some stranger they don't even know just got to third base in front of a whole line of people."

He chuckled, a deep, rumbling sound that reverberated in her chest.

"Ah, they were just doing their jobs. You're good now?" She nodded.

"All right, then. You have a good flight," he said, another flash of his pearly whites sending a tingle through her.

She fidgeted with the strap of her bag, vaguely ashamed of her reaction to him. *He's married!* And definitely not the type of man who would fit in at her parents' country club.

Just the fact she'd thought that made her cringe. Those were her mother's issues running through her head. Not hers. Still, he was off-limits in every possible way. He didn't wear a ring, which was odd. But then, some men didn't. He looked like he worked with his hands. Maybe he couldn't wear a ring for work reasons.

"Thanks," she managed, mustering up a smile.

He nodded with another smile and turned to jog off toward his gate.

Shit! Her flight. She dropped her heels, slipped them on, and took off as fast as she could without actually running. Panic rushed through her and a lifetime of her mother's exhortations for "proper decorum at all times" flew out the window. Cherice slung her bag over her shoulder and hauled ass.

She rounded a corner and passed a woman who had just dropped her bag. The woman had to have been in her eighties and was trying to juggle a rolling suitcase, a carry-on bag, and a purse. The contents of the purse were currently rolling in several directions.

Cherice stopped and went down on her knees to help scoop up the items.

"Oh, thank you, young lady."

"My pleasure," Cherice said, gathering the rest of it up.

"I'm in too big a hurry. My granddaughter is getting married this weekend. I haven't seen her much since she grew up and went off to school. I must be a little excited."

"That sounds wonderful," Cherice said.

It must be nice to actually want to see your family. She shook that thought off and finished cramming everything back in the woman's purse. The woman's carry-on looked half empty. Cherice got the rolling suitcase upright and then asked, "May I?" holding up the purse.

The woman looked confused, but nodded. Cherice opened the carry-on and shoved the purse inside and then draped it so it sat on the suitcase with the straps over the handle.

"It should be a little easier to manage this way."

"Oh, thank you, dear!" The woman patted her cheek. "I better go find my gate."

"Oh crap," Cherice muttered. "I've got to run. It was nice to meet you!" she called over her shoulder.

She didn't dare look at her watch. She just ran for her gate like the walking dead were snapping at her heels.

Chapter Three

Oz had turned when he'd heard the old woman exclaim over her spilled luggage, but before he could go back to help, the attractive woman from the metal detector was already stooping to gather up the grandma's belongings. He didn't know why that surprised him so much. He didn't even know the woman. She could be Mother Theresa for all he knew. But she certainly didn't come across that way. Yet there she was, helping a little old lady and having a grand time chatting while she was doing it from all appearances, despite being late for her plane.

Shit! The plane. Assured that no one needed his help, he jogged to the gate, but shouldn't have bothered. By the time he got to the gate, it was nearly deserted. The plane still sat there, but the doors were closed.

There had to be a way onto that plane. He sauntered over to the check-in podium and plastered on his most charming smile. He glanced at the attendant's name tag.

"Becky? That's a great name. My favorite aunt is named Becky."

Becky's cheeks flushed and she smiled shyly, not quite meeting his gaze.

"Can I help you, sir?"

"I sure hope so. I'm supposed to be on that plane right there," he said, gesturing to where it still sat at the gate. "I know I'm a few seconds late, but the lines were killer. Is there any way I can go ahead and board? I've got my boarding pass and everything all ready."

Becky's smile faded around the edges. "I'm sorry, sir. But once the doors have closed we can't allow any more passengers on board."

Oz's shoulders slumped but he wasn't done trying yet. "Is it possible to make an exception just this once? I really have to get to New York. I can't miss this flight."

"I'm really sorry, sir, but as I just said, once the doors are closed, they can't be opened again. Security rules."

"Ah, I don't look like a threat to national security, do I?" he asked, flirting so hard he was nearly batting his damn eyelashes. "I really need to make this flight. Isn't there something you can do? I mean, the plane is still just sitting there… surely someone as sweet as you could…"

"Excuse me, I'm sorry." The woman who'd been helping the little old lady elbowed her way around him. "I'm sorry," she said again to him. "Do you mind if I butt in real quick?"

Oz opened his mouth but she didn't wait for his response. "Hi, Becky?" She gave Becky a sugary sweet smile that didn't quite reach all the way to her eyes. "Look, I absolutely cannot miss this flight. My sister is getting married tomorrow. The rehearsal dinner is tonight. My mother has invited half the city. If I'm not there she will, very literally, kill me. Are you sure there's nothing you can do? Maybe there is a supervisor or someone who can help work this out…"

Becky shook her head. "My supervisor won't be able to tell you anything different, ma'am. Once the gates are closed they do not open again. For anyone."

The radio buzzed and Becky held up a finger like she was putting the other woman on mute and answered it.

His mystery woman's jaw dropped at the rude dismissal and she sucked in some deep breaths, probably against the urge to scream if the look on her face was any indication. But the movement also forced a pair of very nicely rounded breasts against the thin silk of her blouse. They drew Oz's gaze like an open can of soda drew bees. In fact, everything about her was very nicely rounded. Her well-tailored slacks revealed gently curving hips and a backside that just begged for attention.

Good God, he needed a date. Come to think of it…how long had it been? He couldn't even remember, which meant it had been far too long. No wonder he was drooling over some strange woman when he should be stressing over his flight. Of course, fixing his attention on her was far more pleasant than thinking about what would happen if he didn't make his interview. So fix it he would. No matter how stuck up she might be, and her rescue of the little old lady a few minutes before seemed to throw a small wrench in that assumption, she was certainly fine to look at.

Of course, she chose that moment to glance over at him and he turned his head so she wouldn't catch him smiling. The quick narrowing of her eyes, however, told him he hadn't been quick enough.

Becky put the radio down and sighed. "It looks like the passengers have to deplane anyway. The flight has been grounded."

"What? Why?" the woman asked, going back to ignoring him completely.

"Due to the weather conditions in New York, La Guardia is experiencing extreme delays. All the flights are being rerouted. Newark and JFK are also affected. I believe there is a hurricane warning in effect. Must be what's causing our little storm here, too."

"When will the flights be running again?"

"I'm not sure, ma'am. Right now, we've been told it will most likely be tomorrow morning."

"What?"

She drew a breath to argue more, but Oz caught the commotion coming from the gate and pointed to the doors. "Here they come."

Passengers started streaming out of the gate doors and scattering through the airport. A great many of them took up positions in line behind them. Becky paled and Oz could nearly see her pulling up her big girl panties to deal with the shit storm behind her.

But the woman next to him looked like she was about to cause another one. Oz jumped in before the shit could really hit the proverbial fan. "I think we are both anxious to get to New York today. Is there any possible way we're getting out of here?"

Becky frowned. "If you'd like me to check for flights into nearby airports…"

"Yes, thank you," the woman said, plastering another smile on her face that looked like it was barely containing the panic. "I *have* to be in New York by this evening, tomorrow afternoon at the latest."

Oz leaned against the counter and tossed in his two cents. "That would be great if you could check on other flights, Becky, thanks."

Becky's lips twitched into a modest smile in response to the mega-watt grin aimed at her. If the clamor of the crowd was any indication, she was about to have a really terrible day. The least he could do was be nice while he started it off.

After a few seconds of typing, Becky's smile faded. "I'm sorry, but with the weather the way it is, there are no flights flying anywhere on the east coast."

"What?" the woman squealed. "That's impossible. It's just a little rain."

"I'm sorry, ma'am. I'm afraid I can't even get you into other airports nearby. The weather is causing havoc up and down the east coast."

Oz watched fascinated as one emotion after another chased across the woman's face. Anger and panic eased into a weird calm, though he had no doubt a whole load of turbulence was seething just below the surface. Well, no point in standing there watching her implode and continue to waste Becky's time. He needed to get to New York and if a plane was out of the question, he was going to hurry and get himself a car. Before everyone else had the same idea.

"Well, if there's nothing you can do, there's nothing you can do," Oz said, shrugging and shoving his hands in his pockets. "Thanks for trying. I'm much obliged."

Much obliged? How could he stand there looking so calm and collected? He'd just lost his flight, too. He winked at her and headed off into the crowd. Cherice fought to keep her nervous breakdown from escaping and scaring all the nice people with her crazy. She closed her eyes and took a deep breath. It wasn't this poor woman's fault the weather was delaying things.

But, she'd never hear the end of this. She was supposed to be there last week. Her parents already thought she was a total screw up. Not smart enough to get into the best medical school like her sister. Or any medical school, for that matter. Or charming enough to get their parents' rich friends to throw money at the family charity like her twin brother. That, at least, was useful. She'd never been anything but a disappointment to her family. Now she couldn't even manage to get from North Carolina to New York.

Well, then.

Her phone rang and she shoved her boarding pass back in her bag and grabbed it. Elliot, her twin brother. He was the only one that didn't make her feel like she'd been adopted… or that she should be sent back where she came from.

"Hey Cher-Bear! You on your way yet?"

Cherice smiled at her brother's nickname for her. He was the only person in her life who had ever called her by anything other than her full name. Her mother didn't believe in nicknames. Felt they were low class. Too personal and informal.

"No, my flight was cancelled."

"Oh shit. Well…do they have you on another one? Mom's going to freak."

Cherice sighed. She was well aware of that. "No.

Apparently the little summer storm we are having here is a major hurricane warning up your way. All the flights into any airport near you are grounded."

"Damn. I was hoping it wouldn't be an issue for you. It isn't too bad for us yet, but Mom is freaking out. If it hasn't blown over by tomorrow morning, I think she'll have a serious breakdown. How soon can you get up here?"

"I don't know. There aren't any more flights until tomorrow at the earliest."

"But that's the day of the wedding!"

"I'm aware of that."

"You're going to have to drive. Rent a car."

The room spun a little at the thought. "You want me to rent a car and drive? All the way to New York? You're joking, right?"

She hated driving. With a bright purple polka-dotted passion. She drove around town, to school and back, to the store, that sort of thing. But she avoided it at all costs if the weather was bad, which, apparently, it would be. Plus, she'd never driven long distance before. In fact, she couldn't remember ever being in a car for longer than it took to get from New York City to her parents' place in the Hamptons, and she'd never made the drive herself. Hell, she'd gotten lost once going to the library four miles from her apartment and that was *with* GPS. She'd never make it 1,000 miles.

The laughter on the other end of the phone made it clear her brother was thinking the same thing. "You still there?"

"Yes. I'm just...processing." And possibly hyperventilating.

More laughter. "Look, Cher-Bear, I know driving freaks you out, but you don't really have another choice. You can do this. It's only like twelve hours. If you start now, you'd be here before midnight. That's not too bad. You wouldn't even have to get a hotel or anything. *And* you'll probably beat the worst of the storm."

Cherice stamped down the rising panic and looked up to find Mr. Hot, Blond and *Married* a few feet away, leaning against the counter at the car rental place, staring at her with a weird little half smile on his unbelievably full lips. She frowned at him and turned around so she couldn't see him.

"Maybe you're right. But it's raining. I can barely drive when the weather is perfect."

"You can do this, Cher-Bear. Just get a car, put on some tunes, and haul ass up here."

"Yeah. Okay. Guess I don't have much of a choice."

Elliot snorted. "Not unless you want to deal with the Momster."

Cherice repressed an actual shudder. "No, thanks. Ugh, fine, I'll rent a car. Hopefully, I don't kill myself on the way up."

"You'll be fine, I promise."

"We'll see," Cherice said, dread filling her at the thought of twelve hours alone in a car, driving unfamiliar roads. "Let's just hope the damn thing has GPS."

Elliot snorted. "Like that'll help. I'll send out a rescue crew if you aren't here by morning, I promise. Love you, sis."

"Love you, too, Smelliot."

She hung up to the sound of his laughter. Her smile faded quickly though when she realized she now had to go rent a car.

"Pull it together, Cherice," she muttered to herself. "It's a car, not an assault tank."

She marched to the counter before her courage failed her. Wannabe Rhett Butler stood a bit to the side filling out some papers, so he'd obviously already been helped. Cherice decided it wouldn't be too big a faux pas to butt her way in while he was busy.

"Hi, I need to rent a car. I don't know what kind of a selection you have, but I definitely need something with GPS. And as much insurance as you can give me and whatever other extras are available. And do your cars have really good tires? Something that won't slide around on wet roads?"

Cherice gave the startled woman a faint smile and then glanced over to the man who stared at her with a *what-the hell-was-that* look that was mirrored on the face of Car Rental Lady.

"I'm sorry. Jennifer?" Cherice added, glancing at the woman's name tag. "I'm just in a bit of a rush, and I'm crazy nervous about driving in the rain."

"Oh, no, that's okay…it's just that we are out of cars."

Cherice's stomach churned. "What do you mean you are out of cars? How can you be out?"

"I'm sorry, ma'am. But with flights being canceled we were cleaned out. He got the last one," she said, nodding at the man next to her.

"Hi," he said.

Cherice just stared at him, panic overriding her brain until there was not a single, solitary thought left in her head.

She opened her mouth to say something and promptly shut it again, her throat growing tight with the sudden urge to cry. This could not be happening.

She stalked over to the row of chairs near the counter and flopped into one, her head dropping into her hands.

"Oh my God, I can't believe this is happening. Just shoot me now. Seriously," she mumbled, fully aware she looked like a crazy person and not giving a hamster's furry hiney.

A pair of scuffed work boots appeared in her line of vision and she looked up.

Mr. Gorgeous Blue Eyes was invading her personal space. Her face was level with his stomach and his shirt did little to hide the solid body underneath. It wasn't skin tight, by any means, but it did fit very, very well. His well-worn jeans rode low on his hips and she had a sudden vision of him padding around her apartment in nothing but those jeans, the corded muscles of his hips disappearing into the soft material. Her breath caught in her throat and she straightened in her chair, pulling her prim and proper manners about her like a shield.

"Can I help you?"

"Sorry, I couldn't help overhear your phone call earlier…"

Cherice raised an eyebrow.

He had the grace to blush a little, though Cherice was positive the slight pink in his cheeks couldn't touch the bright red in hers. He certainly wasn't catching her at her best.

"Well, I've got to get to New York, too. Since I've got the last rental, I just thought, seeing as how we are going the same way…well, if you'd like a ride, I'd be happy to drive you."

Relief flooded through her, followed almost immediately by suspicion. Why would a complete stranger want to be alone in a car with her for twelve hours?

"I'm totally trustworthy, I promise. It's just a long way to drive on my own. Plus, I don't see any point in leaving you stranded here when we're going the same direction."

Her face must still have been radiating *Serial Killer Alert* because he added, "Jennifer there has seen us together and has all my info so she could sic the cops on me if she needed to."

"Don't take this the wrong way, but that *does* make me feel a little better," Cherice said, her mouth pulling into a half smile.

He laughed, his handsome features radiating *Good Guy*. He seemed normal enough. He had a wife and child, so he was probably safe. And it was only twelve hours, less than a day. It suddenly seemed a lot shorter since she wouldn't have to drive. If she tried to drive herself she'd probably end up lost or dead, anyway. Not that she had a choice. Her only other option was probably the bus, if one was even running. She grimaced at the thought. She'd rather skip the trip entirely and face her mother, and *that* was saying something.

"All right," she said, lifting her chin. "You've got yourself a car mate."

Chapter Four

Judging by the look on her face, the woman would rather crawl to New York City on her knees than ride in a car with him, so Oz was kind of surprised she agreed. He hadn't missed the quick perusal she'd done of him while she'd been making up her mind. Oh, part of her, at least, had liked what she'd seen. There'd been a little spark in her tawny eyes, a little hitch in her breath. He knew very well what happened when a woman liked what she saw, and they generally did when they saw him. He wasn't conceited, but he knew he looked good. Long hours of hard work tended to whip a guy's muscles into shape.

He'd seen those looks from women before. But behind the flash of heat in their eyes, there was the disdain. The slight nose wrinkle at the grease stains he'd never be able to get totally out from under his nails. The quick calculation of his net worth going by the worn jeans and cheap T-shirt he wore. The pampered princess in front of him was no different. He was good enough to perform whatever service she required, but the way she grimaced and jutted her chin said that was all he'd ever be good for.

It stung. It always did. But he wasn't one to let his emotions off the leash so he slapped a grin on his face and stuck his hand out.

"I'm Oz, by the way."

"Oz?" She took his hand, her fingers curling into the warmth of his. She left her hand in his longer than was strictly polite, then withdrew them quickly like she realized what she'd done. "Were your parents' fans of *The Wizard of Oz* or something?"

His laugh boomed out. "Naw. My real name is Nathaniel Oserkowski. Kind of a mouthful. Oz suits me better."

She blinked at him and opened her mouth like she was going to respond to that. Then she gave her head a little shake. "I'm Cherice Buchanan Debusshere. Nice to meet you."

Oz blinked at her. "Wow. That's quite a name you got there."

She straightened her shoulders, her face flushing slightly. "They're family names."

He bit his tongue to keep from cracking a joke. She wasn't like the flirty, good-natured women he generally chatted up. Teasing her about her name was probably the wrong way to go about getting to know someone he was about to be confined in a tiny space with for the next twelve hours. But damn, with a name like that, she was probably a stuck-up piece of work.

"Well, Cher…"

"Cherice. Not Cher."

Yep. Totally stuck-up. "Okay then. Cherice. Let's go find our car."

Cherice Buchanan Debusshere. What the hell kind of name was that? The woman was begging for a good tumble. She needed something to loosen her up. Her designer outfit and sky-high heels would look great in a board room but would probably have been miserable on a plane, and wouldn't be much better in a car. Her hair was slicked back into a sophisticated ponytail. He couldn't help but wonder what those chestnut strands would look like flowing over her shoulders, damp from a nice hot shower.

He shook his head, trying to dislodge the image from his mind. Ms. Debusshere didn't seem the type to put one manicured pinkie out of place, let alone go slumming with a guy like him. He should have kept on walking when he'd overheard her phone call. But she had seemed genuinely terrified of having to drive. And they were going to the same place. Besides, twelve hours was a mighty long time to keep himself company. It would be nice to have someone to talk to.

Another glance at Cherice almost changed his mind on that one. She didn't seem like the chatty type. At least not with someone like him. If things had worked out differently in his life, he might have been sitting in one of those fancy offices where women like Cherice worked. He wouldn't be covered in oil from his job as a mechanic at Billy's garage, or have dark circles under his eyes from his second job delivering newspapers in the middle of the night. Or his weekend janitor job.

But he did what he had to do. His sister and nephew needed him and he'd do what it took to provide for them. And if he had to deal with women like Cherice looking down their noses at him, well, it was a small price to pay to see the smile on his nephew's face when he got home from work every day. To see the boy thriving, and healthy, and happy.

Now, however, the perfect opportunity had opened up. He had a shot at his dream job. A long shot, sure. But a shot, nonetheless. If he made it to the interview.

Oz put on his brightest smile and made chit-chat on their way out to the car rental parking lot but Cherice was remarkably hard to draw out. Until she saw their car.

"What is that?"

"A Ford Focus."

"Do they have a more recent model? The newer cars tend to have better safety features, don't they? It's raining and it's supposed to rain all day. That means the roads will be slippery."

"I'm sure this one is safe. As long as we don't go off-roading or anything like that, it should be fine."

She frowned, chewing on her lip. "It has GPS, right?"

"Yep. And we've got enough insurance on it we could drive it off a cliff and get reimbursed. Is it okay?" he asked. It wasn't like she had a choice, but he figured it didn't hurt to ask. Maybe he'd get lucky and she'd decide she didn't want a ride after all.

"Of course," she said with a small smile. "Does it have all-weather tires?"

"Yes, ma'am."

"Oh good. Do you mind if I ask a few more questions?" Twenty minutes later, Oz stood watching while Cherice worried about every safety hazard she could think of and asking the poor car rental guy to reassure her. He'd known she was

nervous, but she was crossing the line into paranoia. As long
as the car wasn't going to blow up when he turned it on, he
was cool with it. His phone buzzed and he took it out, smiling at the cute picture of his nephew that his sister texted
him.

R U in the air yet?

He grimaced. *Flight canceled. Gonna drive.*

Oh no! U r driving the whole way? B careful!

*No worries. Sharing the car. I won't fall asleep with
her sitting next to me.*

Her? Do tell ;-)

Oz snorted. *Lol. Don't even. There will never be anything
to "tell" with her.*

You say that now…

He glanced up to watch Cher buzzing around the car,
her face creased with concern while the attendant continued
to assure her everything was fine. *No…believe me. She's a
serious piece of work. And not in the good way.*

If you say so…

I say so :-)

*Drive safe. And check in at some point so I know you
aren't dead in a ditch somewhere.*

LOL will do. Love ya! Give Tyler a hug for me.

Will do <3

"I think I've alleviated most of her concerns, sir."

"Sorry," Oz muttered, holding out his hand for the keys.

The attendant just walked away, shaking his head.

"All right, then," Oz said, sliding into the driver's seat. "Let's get this show on the road."

Cherice slipped into the passenger seat. Oz started the car and got his mirrors and seat adjusted while she buckled up and arranged herself. He turned on the radio and bobbed his head to the song pouring from the speakers. Ah, "Lowrider." Excellent driving tune.

He pulled out of the lot and wound through the lanes of the airport leading to the freeway, singing the lyrics and lightly tapping his hands on the steering wheel along to the beat. His shoulders relaxed, the tension starting to drain out of him.

Oz merged into traffic and turned the volume down in case she wanted to pass the time by chatting. Apparently, she didn't. After five minutes of dead silence, he couldn't take it anymore. Did she really plan on just sitting there for the whole trip, not saying a word?

"So, why are you going to New York?"

She glanced at him for a moment before turning back to look out her window. "My older sister's wedding."

"Oh, that's great. Family gatherings are always a blast."

"Depends on the family," she murmured.

Before he could dig into that kettle of worms, she lobbed his question back at him. "Why are you going to New York?"

"Job interview."

"In New York?"

The incredulity in her voice was downright offensive, no matter what kind of spin you put on it.

"Why? You don't think a grease monkey like me would make it in New York?"

"I didn't say that."

"You didn't have to."

She sighed. "I didn't mean to offend you. It just surprises me, that's all. New York is a long way from North Carolina."

"That's true enough. So what are you doing out in the sticks if your family is in New York?"

She paused for a moment, her full bottom lip caught between her teeth. *Hmmm*, princess wasn't too keen on answering that question, huh? Interesting.

"I went to school at Duke. I was going to go to grad school but…that didn't work out. So I just kind of…stayed."

"Why didn't grad school work out?"

She blew out a breath and turned to look at him, exasperation stamped clear on her face. "I was trying to get into a pre-med program."

"Really?"

"What, you don't think a girl like me can make it in med school?"

He didn't think it wise, or nice anyway, to say that, no, he didn't think she'd make it in a medical program. She sat there in her perfectly put together outfit, not a hair out of place, with her soft, manicured hands that were as smooth as the day she'd come into the world. So picturing her up to her elbows in body fluids at the beck and call of the infirm? Yeah, he didn't think so. But kudos to her for getting his own words to bite him in the ass.

"Touché," he said, laughing.

A little shiver ran through her and her hand clenched on her thigh. Well, well. The spittin' kitten wasn't as unaffected by him as she liked to pretend. This could be fun.

"I didn't mean to offend you," he said, echoing her words back to her. "You just…"

She faced him, her eyes narrowing. "I just what?"

He shrugged. "Don't seem the medical type."

"You don't even know me."

"Very true. So, let's get to know each other. We got a long trip ahead of us. Might as well make some conversation."

"You're awful chatty for a guy."

He raised an eyebrow. "I am?"

She looked back out at the raindrops that had started hitting the windshield again. "Chatting up a perfect stranger isn't how most guys I know would want to spend their mornings."

"Well, most guys you know probably don't find themselves alone in a tiny space with a perfect stranger with nothing else to do for the next twelve hours, either."

Her lips twitched. "Touché," she muttered.

Oz almost fist bumped the air in triumph. The princess had a funny bone, after all. Well, a little one, anyway. A knuckle, maybe.

"So."

Her eyes narrowed again. "So, what?"

"Tell me about yourself."

"There's not much to tell."

"Ah, I don't believe that."

She sighed. "Why don't you tell me about yourself?"

"I asked you first."

"I thought only children used that argument."

Oz shrugged. "I live with a child. He must have rubbed off on me. So spill it. Tell me about your family. Are you excited for your sister's wedding? Or do you have family drama? What do you guys usually do for Christmas?"

"Look, Nathaniel—"

"I prefer Oz."

"I prefer Nathaniel."

"Seriously? It's *my* name."

"But *I'm* the one who has to say it."

Fire flashed in those golden eyes of hers and parts of Oz that shouldn't be interested perked up and said *hello*. No doubt about it, he definitely preferred the hellcat to the prim and proper routine. He must be out of his mind.

"What? You don't like nicknames?"

The fire bled out of her eyes and she looked back out the window. "No. They are lo…too personal and informal."

Hmm. He'd be willing to bet those weren't her words coming out of her mouth. As irritating as the woman was, even her prim and proper attitude was better than this somehow sad, resigned quietness. He wanted the kitty to show her claws again.

"So why didn't grad school work out? You aren't going for pre-med anymore?"

Cher straightened, every muscle visibly on edge, like a rubber band that someone was stretching to its breaking point. "No."

"Why not?"

She sighed, the same loud, exasperated exhale that his sister made whenever he was being a pest. The similarity made him smile, which didn't win him any points with Cher. Cherice. Whatever she wanted to be called. Her eyes narrowed. "My undergrad grades were decent but I totally bombed the MCATs, okay? I'd really rather not talk about it."

Touchy, touchy. "All right, then. So…what are you doing now?"

"What do *you* do? And don't you dare say you asked me first. I shared. It's your turn."

"All right, all right. Fair's fair. I'm a mechanic mostly. And on the weekends, I work as a janitor at the community college."

"Oh. That's nice."

That's nice? It was painfully obvious she had no idea how to respond. He was probably the first mechanic/janitor she'd ever met.

"Your turn again. Why didn't you go back home after you…once you were done with school?"

She was quiet enough he wasn't sure she'd answer him. She kept her gaze on the rain trailing down her window, but she finally did. "Because crawling back home to listen to my perfect family repeatedly tell me what a failure I am didn't seem like a fun thing to do."

"I'm sure they would have been supportive. They love you, right?"

"Look, no offense, Nathaniel—"

"Oz."

"Oh my god, Nathaniel, Oz, whatever. Ox is a more fitting a nickname if you insist on one."

"Why, am I stubborn or something?" he said, chuckling.

Her lips twitched into a reluctant smile. "Yeah, or something."

"Looked in a mirror lately?"

Cher's smile grew wider and she ducked her head. "Look, I'd rather not talk about my family right now, if it's all the same to you. Ox."

"Nag."

Her eyes widened. "Excuse me?"

"Nag. You know. From the movie with Walter Matthau and Sophia Loren. She calls him Ox, he calls her Nag."

She just blinked at him like he was speaking a foreign language.

"Never mind. You've probably never seen it."

"I've seen it," she said, finally speaking.

She just didn't think *he* had. Got it. Oz gripped the steering wheel a little tighter and tried to let it go. "What's with the attitude about your family?"

Her jaw dropped and the spark was back in her eyes. "I don't have an attitude about them."

"Yes, you do. Your whole body goes rigid every time I mention them."

"No, it doesn't."

"Yes, it does," he said, running a finger down Cher's arm. The warm flesh beneath his finger trembled until she jerked away. "See. Every muscle in your body is clenched."

"They are not. And stop looking at my body." Her voice was annoyed, but a blush crept up her cheeks and she wouldn't meet his eyes.

He let a slow, seductive smile spread across his lips, before turning his attention back to the road. "I'm not looking. I was just using an example."

"Whatever."

The small caveman part of him pounded his chest that

he could affect her even though she seemed to be trying so hard to keep her distance. Then again, it didn't really matter if she liked him or not. A girl like her would never stoop low enough to be interested in a guy like him.

Which left egging her on the only option.

"So…" he said.

"So, what?"

"Come on, spill the beans."

Her mouth dropped open. "Seriously, you have no filter, do you?"

He just grinned at her. She stared at him, her eyes narrowed, mouth slightly open…sort of like a monkey doing a math problem. Then she leaned over and turned the volume up on the stereo. Lynyrd Skynyrd blared from the speakers.

"You like this song?" he asked.

"Yep." She turned her gaze out her window, shutting him out as effectively as she could without actually jumping from the moving vehicle.

Oz snorted and leaned back, getting comfortable while he rocked out.

"Oh! We need to stop," he said, checking traffic behind him so he could pull the car over to the side of the road.

"What? Why? We've only been on the road for like…" She checked her watch. "Thirty minutes. Barely. Is something wrong with the car?"

Oz pointed out the window at the Welcome to Tennessee sign. "No. But I wanna take pictures at all the state-line signs so I can send them to Tyler."

The annoyance faded from her face, replaced by that soft *aw how cute* look women often got when men did something child related. That look usually made him nervous—the last thing he wanted was a baby-hungry woman throwing goo-goo eyes at him. At least at that exact moment in his life. But if it would get Cher to take his picture, he was happy to exploit it.

"How about I just hang out the window and take it so only one of us is getting wet," she said, grimacing through the windows at the rain splattering down.

"Deal." He handed her his phone and grabbed the door handle. "Ready?"

She rolled down her window enough to get an unobstructed shot of the sign and nodded. "Go for it."

Oz jumped out of the car, ran to the sign and struck a goofy pose.

The flash went off but before he could run back to the car she called out. "Hang on! It's all blurry. Do it again."

He sighed and shoved his now sopping hair out of his face and posed again. She held the phone up but no flash went off.

"Did you take it?" he called.

"You keep moving, hold still."

He frowned. "I'm not moving. Just take it!"

"Well now you're frowning. Smile."

He grinned, though it was more like gritting his teeth. She turned the phone horizontally like she was going for a better angle. Then turned it back vertical.

"Take the picture!" he said.

The flash finally went off.

"Did you get it that time?" he asked.

"Yeah, I got it." She lowered the phone and he caught sight of the little smile she failed to wipe from her face.

Oh. So she wanted to play games? Keep him standing

in the pouring rain so he got totally soaked? Well then, it would be only fair to give her something to look at for all her troubles.

Oz got to the driver's side but didn't get in the car right away. Instead, he whipped off his shirt, letting the rain run in rivulets down the muscles of his chest while he made a big show of wringing it out. He leaned in to chuck the shirt into the backseat and then straightened up, arching his back a little while he ran both hands through his hair, getting all the wet strands from his face.

He finally slid back into the car. Cher stared at him, her face flushed and her mouth hanging open. He leaned across her, his own grin on his face while he opened the glove box and dug around.

She made a little "eep!" sound and pressed herself back against her seat.

"You're getting me all wet!" she said.

Oz closed his eyes briefly, an altogether different context for that phrase invading his mind. She had no idea how wet he could get her if he really tried. God, it really *had* been too long since he'd had a date. He'd have to remedy that when he got back from this little road trip from hell.

"Just looking for some napkins or something to dry off," he explained.

"Well, if you'll move, I have some tissues in my purse…"

He grinned at her and sat back, taking his time to retreat back to his side of the car. She glared at him but reached down and snagged her purse from the floorboard, retrieving a small packet of travel tissues from its depths. She tossed them at him.

He extracted a few and made another show of wiping

the water from his skin. She watched for a second, a sigh escaping that full mouth of hers. His smile widened and she blinked, apparently figuring out that she'd been ogling him. She glared at him again and moved back as far as she could against her door, her arms crossed over her chest while she kept her gaze firmly glued to the view outside her window.

Oz chuckled and finished drying himself off. He leaned over into the backseat and rummaged in his bag for a spare T-shirt. Cher visibly relaxed once he'd pulled it over his head.

"Here," she said, handing him back his phone. He checked out the picture.

"A little blurry but it'll work. One down, six more to go."

"Six?" she asked, shocked.

"Yup. We just got Tennessee. Virginia is about forty more minutes up the road. Then West Virginia, Maryland, Pennsylvania, New Jersey, and New York."

Cher leaned back against her headrest and closed her eyes. "Fantastic."

Oz snorted. Oh yeah. This trip was going to be a riot.

Chapter Five

Cherice woke when the car pulled to a stop. She blinked and peeled her face away from the window, looking in horror at the streak of what had to be drool that had crusted to the glass. She wiped her mouth, hoping Nathaniel hadn't noticed. Not that she cared what he thought of her or anything. But still. Gross.

"I need a pit stop," he said, opening his door.

"A what?"

"Bathroom break. If you want any snacks or need a bathroom run, you might want to do it now. Unless you want to go somewhere and grab some lunch?"

She stepped out of the car and looked around the tiny town. At least she assumed it was a town. It was green and beautiful like everything else they'd passed, but aside from the ramshackle gas station they'd pulled into, there was nothing else in sight except for an old farmhouse in the distance and a few rundown shops across the street. And damn, it was *hot*. She pulled off the thin sweater that covered her shoulders, leaving on just the silk shell and she fanned herself with her hand. But that did nothing at all to cool her off.

"*Is* there anywhere around here to get anything to eat? Where are we?"

Nathaniel glanced around. "Somewhere in the middle of Virginia. There was a diner not too far back. And I'm sure we can find a McDonald's or something up the road somewhere."

Cherice repressed a shudder. "I think I'll just see what I can find in there."

Nathaniel shrugged. "Suit yourself."

He leaned back, bending far enough to pop his back, exposing a nicely muscled strip of toned belly at the same time. Her eyes zeroed in on that deliciously taut skin, her mind happily fixating on the memory of what other bits of goodness were hiding under his shirt, before she made herself look away. She had no business drooling on him. Over him! She meant *over* him. An uncomfortably warm breeze whipped through the station and ruffled Nathaniel's light brown hair. Cherice had the sudden urge to run her fingers through it, find out if it was as soft as it looked. The thought was immediately followed by a rush of shame so strong her cheeks burned with it. The man was *married*. Her neglected libido really needed to get that important fact wrapped around its head.

He looked over his shoulder and caught her staring at him. Those eyes of his...Cherice couldn't help but fall into them. She couldn't pinpoint the exact color. Blue, yes. But darker than cornflower blue. Not quite sapphire. Almost a blue-gray. She wondered if his eyes changed colors depending on what he wore.

His forehead creased a little in confusion, but when she didn't drop her gaze right away he gave her a small smile. Cherice blinked, the smile shaking her out of whatever mind haze she was in. They'd been on the road just a few hours and he was already an almost constant thought running through her head. In her defense, concentrating on the lovely male specimen before her was a lot better than dwelling on the miserable weekend ahead of her. But seeing as how the object of her obsession was married, she really needed to rein in it. She tore her gaze from his and ran her hand over her hair, making sure it was still firmly captured in the ponytail.

"I'm going to run inside. Are you coming?"

Cherice shook her head and pulled out her phone. "I need to check some emails real quick."

"All right. I'll be back in a few."

She nodded, not really paying attention as she scrolled through a few emails from work, one or two from friends, and a cat video or two. She responded to the ones that needed responding to and then put her phone away, reaching into the backseat to grab her suitcase so she could put her sweater away. Despite the rain, the air hung hot and heavy. The sweater wouldn't be needed any time soon. The zipper jammed when she tried to open it and she had to get out of the car to drag it out and prop it up on the trunk instead.

Cherice tugged on the zipper but it didn't budge. It had jammed enough that she couldn't zip the thing back up or unzip it fully. And it was enough of a pain, she was about ready to give it up. One more try. Maybe if she propped it on its side so she could tug downward, it would give her a little better leverage.

She tilted the case on the end of the trunk so she could yank without slamming her hand into the car. She got a good grip on the zipper and tugged with all her strength. It finally gave. But she tugged too hard and the momentum followed through, jerking the suitcase right off the car.

"Cher, be care—"

The lid swung wide, spilling the contents out onto the wet asphalt. Nathaniel hurried over, his hands full of hot dogs and bags of junk food.

Cherice ignored him and dove for her clothes. Half of them had landed in a puddle, the other half on the wet and filthy ground.

Nathaniel left his stuff on the trunk and helped her gather everything up. She scrambled around, trying to scoop everything up before it was completely ruined. What was wrong with her? Why did everything she touch have to turn into such an unmitigated disaster? A pair of panties had fluttered beneath the car and she gingerly reached for them.

If she looked up and Nathaniel was laughing she'd hitchhike the rest of the way to New York. But he wasn't laughing. In fact, when she finally pulled away from the car, her undies wadded in her hand, it was to find that he'd repacked her suitcase as best he could. He'd even emptied one of his bags from the mini-mart to keep the clothes that were totally soaking wet from dripping all over everything else.

"Thanks," she said, accepting his help to stand up.

His large hand wrapped around hers and he pulled her to her feet. If it had been appropriate, she might have cuddled into his well-muscled chest and let him hold her. She could use a hug. And from the electric heat spreading through her at the mild contact of his hand on hers, she was willing to bet a hug would feel a million times better.

But it *wasn't* appropriate. So she pulled her hand from his grasp and stepped back. Right into the puddle.

The murky water splashed half way up her calf. Some greasy substance oozed around her ankle and leaked into her shoe and she swallowed her revulsion. The skin on her foot crawled like it was trying to get away from the nastiness coating it.

She closed her eyes and took a deep breath.

A choked-off laugh sent a hot streak of anger burning through her chest. The inappropriate thoughts of cuddling were crowded out by even more inappropriate thoughts of a more violent nature. She lifted her foot out of the puddle, shaking it off as she turned to look at Nathaniel. He covered his mouth, trying to change his laugh into a cough.

Her eyes narrowed and she clenched her fists against the sudden urge to lob the nearest chunk of garbage at him.

"Watch out for that puddle," he said.

"You couldn't have said something a minute earlier?"

"Sorry. But since we just dug your clothes out of it, I figured you knew it was there," he said, his voice cracking on another laugh.

She couldn't tell him she hadn't been paying attention because she'd been too distracted by the warm tingles running up her arm from where he'd touched her. So she blurted the first thing that came to mind. "These are $500 shoes! My mother gave them to me for my birthday; they're almost brand new."

His eyes widened. "Well for that much money, you'd think they'd be waterproof."

Even though that was funny, she wasn't going to give him

the satisfaction of a laugh. Besides, if she opened her mouth to respond she'd let loose a string of curses that would make a sailor proud. Her anger was a great shield against the attraction she couldn't help feeling for him. Maybe if she could stay pissed at him the entire journey she could keep her impure thoughts at bay.

She shook her foot again and stomped off toward the station. She could feel his eyes on her as she picked her way across the asphalt. Once inside she found the ladies room, only to discover the door was locked. Cherice marched over to the counter. The man on duty barely glanced up from his paper.

"Excuse me," she said, trying very hard to hold onto her temper.

"Yeah?"

"I'd like to use the restroom, but it is locked."

The cashier handed her a key attached to a hubcap without looking up again. "Make sure you return that."

The thing weighed ten pounds at least. She wasn't likely to run off with it, though, that was probably the idea. She'd definitely never imagined when she woke up this morning that she'd be begging a gas station attendant for permission to use a bathroom that required a key with a chain bobble larger than her head. She forced a polite smile.

This day was just one clusterfuck of a disaster after another. She didn't see how it could get any worse.

Until she walked into what passed for a bathroom in whatever godforsaken town she was in. To be fair, she'd never been in a gas-station bathroom before, so she really had no comparison for it. Growing up, they'd always flown on their family vacations and she tended to stay pretty close to home since she was on her own. A gas-station pit stop had just never come up before. But she thought it might be better to pee in the woods than it would be to attempt to use facilities that looked like they hadn't been cleaned since Reagan was in the White House.

There were paper towels and running water, at least. She dropped the key with its makeshift keychain on the floor, grabbed some paper towels, and turned on the faucet. The water turned on with such force it ricocheted out of the basin and all over the whole front of her white silk tank.

Cherice swallowed past the sudden lump in her throat. If there was a God, she must have seriously pissed Him off.

She tried the water again, this time just barely turning the knob. The water trickled out in a steady stream and she wet her paper towels, then set to attacking the muddy stain on her pant leg. After five minutes of careful dabbing and downright scrubbing with soap and water, she had to concede defeat. The stain wasn't coming off.

Her foot was dry, at least. Except now her right high heel was three shades darker than the left. Since the rest of the clothes she'd packed were now filthy, wet, or both, she'd have to find some place along the road to replace them. Right now, she'd be a shoe-in for any wet T-shirt contest this side of the Mississippi. If she walked into her parents' house looking the way she did now they probably wouldn't even let her in the front door.

Now. For the other pressing matter. She took another look at the toilet and decided she could hold it a while longer.

Her bladder, however, disagreed.

She sighed. "Damn it."

There was no getting out of there until she'd taken care

of business, but she wasn't sitting on *that* either. Two minutes of generously layering toilet paper over every inch of
exposed porcelain, employing the tried-and-true *squat and
hover* technique, nearly crying with relief when she remembered the tissue in her pocket (because of course, she'd used
all the TP in the bathroom to create her commode barrier),
and she was out of there. Foot reinserted into her squishy,
wet heel, bladder relieved, she was in firm resolve from that
point on to hold it until she reached New York.

She left the bathroom, dropped the hub-cap key back on
the counter, and headed outside. The hot air hitting her wet
shirt created an instant sauna effect that had perspiration
rolling down her back within seconds. Cherice took great
care to walk around the sinkhole of death on her way to
the car. Nathaniel waited inside, stuffing his face with some
disgusting-looking hot dog smothered in ketchup.

She climbed in and aimed the air vents in her direction.
The blast of icy air made her nipples pucker against the
wet material of her shirt, something she didn't realize was
noticeable until Nathaniel stopped in mid bite and stared
like…well, like he'd just noticed a pair of nipples pressing
against a wet, white shirt.

"Problems?" he asked.

"If you must know, I had a little mishap with the water
faucet."

Nathaniel's lips twitched but he wisely didn't laugh
again. He put his hot dog on the dashboard and reached
into the backseat. He unzipped his suitcase and rummaged
through what little was in there. From what she could tell,
there was only a pair of slacks and a white polo shirt, a black
T-shirt, and…heat rushed to her cheeks and she turned back

around. Apparently, Mr. Oserkowski was a boxer-briefs man. She started reciting the Pledge of Allegiance to keep the image of him wearing nothing but his underwear out of her head. He pulled out the black shirt.

"Here. You can wear this."

"Thank yo—oh you have got to be kidding me," she said, catching sight of what was on the shirt.

"Sorry," Nathaniel said with a huge grin, not looking the least bit sorry. "A buddy of mine got it for me as a gag gift but it's really comfortable. I was going to wear it on the way home."

The black shirt had a picture of a man in a chef's hat, holding tongs and standing next to a grill with the words "Once you put your meat in my mouth you're going to want to swallow."

"I can't wear *this* in public!"

"Why not?"

She just stared at him, mouth hanging open.

He released a long suffering breath. "Fine. Give it here."

He grabbed the neck of his T-shirt and before Cherice could say another word, yanked it off, treating her to an eye-ful of visual yumminess. His broad shoulders sloped into a chest that was lightly dusted with hair and solid enough to prove he either worked out or worked hard on a regular ba-sis. His pale nipples were rock hard in the breeze of the air conditioner, and Cherice had to bite her lip against the urge to lean forward and warm one with her tongue.

Married, married, married, she chanted over and over in her head. She frowned. "What is with you? Are you physi-cally incapable of keeping your clothes on?"

His eyebrows raised, his lips pulling into a half smile.

"Only around some people." He held out his blue T-shirt, but she was too stunned by the sudden peep-show to take it. "You can't sit there all day in wet clothes. You can wear my shirt for now."

"Oh. No, thank you. I couldn't…"

"Yes, you can. It's…" He glanced down at her perk and alert breasts. "Distracting…"

She gasped and slapped her hands over her chest. He chuckled and took the offensive gag-gift shirt, raising his arms to slip it on. She got another quick glimpse of washboard abs and a trail to what she was sure was a very ample treasure disappearing into the band of his jeans. Then the shirt he'd removed hit her in the face, enveloping her in the warmth leftover from his body and the scent of some strong, pine-based soap, along with a hint of motor oil. And damn, if that wasn't the manliest thing she'd ever smelled in her life.

"Thank you…but how am I supposed to…I mean…"

"Just switch them out real quick. There's no one here but me. And I promise I won't look."

Sure. She'd heard that one before. Well, she hadn't, but still… Cherice muttered a quick curse under her breath and looked out the window to make sure no one was about.

"Turn your head," she ordered him.

He rolled his eyes but did as she asked. She whipped her wet tank over her head and pulled his shirt on as fast as she could. She nearly groaned in pleasure as the material settled over her. The shirt drowned her, but she snuggled into it, thankful to be dry again.

"Good to go?"

She nodded and put her seat belt on.

He grabbed his hot dog—at least she thought it was

a hot dog. It was covered in too many condiments to tell for sure. Sausage, maybe. Meatballs? Whatever it was, he sank his teeth into it with a moan of pleasure that put more naughty thoughts into her head until she focused on the oozing pile of vinegary slop on top of it. He chewed, oblivious to her revulsion, pulling out of the gas station and back onto the road.

"That is so disgusting. I don't know how you can eat that."

"It's delicious. Didn't you get any snacks?"

"No, I wasn't hungry."

"You sure? Unless you want to get some lunch somewhere it might be a while before we stop again."

"I'm sure."

"Okay." He leaned over and rummaged through his bag. "Here." He handed her a water bottle and a granola bar. "Just in case."

"Thanks." She was a little hungry, but the thought of eating anywhere within a fifty-mile radius of the cesspit of a gas station made her stomach curl into the fetal position.

"You sure you don't want a bite?" he asked, waving the mystery meat in her face again.

"No," she said, firmly shoving it back at him. "Thank you. It's revolting."

"Ah, how do you know if you won't try it?" He shoved it at her again. "You haven't eaten all day. You've got to be hungry." He waved it under her nose. The vinegar stench of the ketchup, and whatever else was mixed in, made her stomach turn. Since it didn't seem to be raining so hard right now, she rolled down the window, hoping the fresh air would help.

"Do you have to wave it in my face?"

"I don't have to…"

"Are you amusing yourself?"

"A little bit, yeah," he said, aiming for her nose again.

The smell hit her again and she grimaced. She batted at his hand and a huge dollop of ketchup landed with a plop right on her chest.

Nathaniel froze for a second, then smiled with sheepish vindication. Like he was happy she'd gotten smeared but felt bad about being happy. "I'm sorry," he said. "I didn't mean to spill on you."

Cherice closed her eyes and leaned her head back against the headrest. She wondered what Nathaniel would do if she opened the door and just jumped out. It might be preferable to riding the rest of the way to New York in the same car with him. It was definitely preferable to what she'd deal with once she got to New York.

"That's okay," she said, perking up a bit. "It's *your* shirt."

"Ah damn."

Cherice had the almost overwhelming urge to stick her tongue out and say "nee-ner nee-ner," but she managed to keep it to a smug grin.

"Here," he said, handing her a travel pack of baby wipes.

"Where did you get those?"

"I grabbed some at the gas station. I always carry some with me. Very handy."

Her heart fluttered a little. He carried baby wipes with him. That was ridiculously cute. And the reason he carried them was probably for his son and she had no right to be fluttering over anything Nathaniel related.

She cleaned herself up as best she could. Good thing the

shirt wasn't hers because there was no saving it. Something mixed into the condiments was greasy and lingering. A more pressing issue was the faint leftover vinegar smell that was mixing with the baby-powder scent of the wipes into a noxious cocktail of fumes that made her already wobbly stomach balk. The icky squishiness in her shoe wasn't helping. She took it off, wiped it down with a baby wipe until it was as clean as she could get it, and then hung it out the window.

"What are you doing?"

"Drying my shoe. It got soaked in parking-lot water."

"It's going to start raining again."

"So I'll bring it back in when it starts."

"You're going to drop it."

"No, I won't."

Nathaniel shrugged. Cher leaned her head back against the head rest and closed her eyes.

"Are we there yet?" she muttered.

Nathaniel's laugh turned to a curse and the car jerked to the side and then bounced over a pot hole. Cher's hand smacked against the door of the car, knocking her heel out of her hand. She shrieked and brought her hand back inside the car, sans shoe.

"You did that on purpose!"

"I didn't, I swear. I didn't even see the pot hole."

"Yeah, right."

"I told you you were going to drop it."

"And then you made sure I did!"

"I didn't tell you to hang your shoe out the window. In fact, if you'll recall, I told you *not* to do that."

"You…I…*grrrr*." She sat back and crossed her arms over her chest, wondering how much prison time she'd get if she took the other shoe and clubbed him with it. "Don't talk to me."

Nathaniel's lips twitched. If he laughed she was going to do it, and to hell with the consequences. She doubted any judge would convict her.

"Suit yourself," he said.

She ignored him and turned around in her seat to dig into her suitcase for her spare pair of shoes. Her specially ordered wedding shoes, dyed to match her dress, and adorned with a rhinestone peacock feather, still sat nestled in her luggage. But dig as she might, she could only locate one of her other shoes. She closed her eyes with a groan.

"You didn't happen to pick up another shoe that looks like this one when we were repacking my bag, did you?"

Oz glanced at it. "Nope. I only picked up clothes. No shoes."

Cherice focused on drawing long, slow breaths into her lungs. No way did she just pull a Cinderella at some godforsaken gas station in the middle of nowhere.

"What's the problem?" Oz asked. "You didn't grab it, either?"

"No. What am I supposed to do without shoes?"

"Don't you have more in your suitcase?"

"Just the shoes for the wedding. And there's no way I'm wearing those. My mother had to special order them to match the bridesmaid's dresses. If they get ruined, she'll kill me. So all I've got is the one heel I've got on and this," she said, holding up a black patent-leather ballet flat.

"So just wear one of each."

"Seriously?"

"What?" he asked, his face a total blank. Either he was

an incredible poker player, or he really had no clue why his suggestion was ridiculous.

"I could probably overlook the fact that they are different colors, but since you obviously didn't notice, *this* one," she said holding up her foot as best she could, "has a four-inch heel and *this* one is a flat!"

"And?"

"Nathaniel!"

"Oz."

She gripped the shoe to keep from throwing it at his head. It wouldn't be good to bean the guy driving the car. "Don't start with that again!"

Nathaniel grinned at her and reached back to rummage in his magic bag again. "Here."

He tossed a pair of men's size-fourteen flip flops on her lap.

"You've got to be joking."

He shrugged. "Better than nothing."

"Why do you even have these?"

"I always wear flip flops in hotel showers. Don't you?"

Cherice released a long, slow breath and cracked open the water bottle, wishing it was something a lot stronger. She only took just enough of a sip to wet her mouth. Better ration it. The last thing in the world she needed was another bathroom break.

Chapter Six

Oz threw his snack trash into the bag from the gas station and took a swig of his water. Cherice hadn't said a word since the untimely demise of her shoe. But she had managed to nearly pick a hole in his shirt before giving up and going back to sleep. He tried to shy away from thoughts of clothing. The quick glimpse of lace-covered breast he'd seen was a sight he wouldn't forget any time soon. And she looked downright adorable swimming in his shirt. Too bad that adorable package was wrapped around a seriously annoying woman who smelled like a diaper-changing station at a ballpark. Ketchup and baby powder…not a great combo.

He didn't know what this woman's deal was but something was eating her up in the worst way. Maybe that was why she was so prickly. The only time she didn't look like she was about to vomit from stress was when she was firing off barbs at him. Except when she was staring out the window trying to ignore the fact that he existed. Or pretending like she hadn't enjoyed the glimpses she'd seen of his body. He had half a mind to make the rest of the trip shirtless, just to watch her squirm. It was certainly muggy enough to justify a bit of stripping.

She finally sat up, blinking her eyes at him.

"Hey," he said.

She gave him a faint smile, then turned her head and wiped at her mouth.

He laughed. "No drool this time."

Her cheeks blushed but she ignored that comment. "Where are we now?"

"Almost to West Virginia."

"Ah, finally. I didn't think it would take so long to get across Virginia."

Oz snorted. "Yeah, it's bigger than it looks on the map."

"Yeah," she said, turning her attention back to the same scenery they'd been seeing for the last six or so hours. Lush green interspersed with towns, homes, and shopping centers, all seen through a hazy, watery filter.

Cher didn't seem inclined to continue their conversation. He didn't know if she was still pissed over her shoe or what, but he had no intention of sitting silent for the rest of the trip. Hell, one of the reasons he'd wanted her along in the first place was so he didn't have to drive alone with nothing but the radio to keep him company.

"So what have you been doing since the med-school plan didn't work out?"

She let a little sigh go and turned to him. "You don't have to make conversation with me, you know. I'm fine just sitting here."

"Well, I'm not. It's a long way to New York and talking

will help keep me awake and alert. Unless you want to take a turn."

She looked out the window at the cars whizzing by in the rain and shook her head. That's what he thought.

She sighed. "Fine."

"Did you even want to be a doctor?"

"It's kind of the family business. It seemed like a good idea to follow in their footsteps," she answered quietly.

"What about nursing?"

Cherice gave a short laugh. "Not prestigious enough for a Debusshere. My father and grandfather are plastic surgeons. My sister is a—"

"Plastic surgeon?"

She shook her head. "Cardiologist."

"Ah. Mother?"

"Lawyer. A very successful one. Until she married my father. She now runs the Debusshere family. Very successfully."

"Tough crew to live up to."

"Yes," she said quietly.

"So, what are you doing now?"

Her chin went up a few notches. Ah, she was gearing up for battle. This should be good then.

"I…sort of help people shop."

"What? Like one of those personal shoppers?"

"Something like that."

"Is that something that a lot of people need?" He tried not to sound too condescending, but seriously? She shopped for other people for a living?

"Yes, it is something that some people need. I started doing this kind of thing back in high school through our Key Club. One day, during my sophomore year at Duke, I got lost driving around and sort of stumbled across a similar organization to the one I'd volunteered for back then. They were looking for help and it had always been something I'd enjoyed and was good at. I mostly work with women who are trying to reenter the workforce. It's not always easy knowing how to dress, what to buy. I help them do that. I also do a little freelance work—shopping for whatever my clients need."

Oz wasn't sure what to say for a second. That had to be the most frivolous, ridiculous occupation for a grown woman he'd ever heard of.

"I know what you're thinking," she said.

"I didn't say a word."

She huffed, her lips pulling into a frown. "You didn't have to. I've heard it all from my parents, believe me."

"You can't get mad at me for something I didn't even say."

"Just because someone like you wouldn't understand my line of work doesn't mean I don't provide a valuable service."

"Someone like me?"

Her cheeks flushed, the heat spreading clear down her neck. "I just meant…I mean, I didn't mean anything bad. I just meant that you…you're not…I mean as a man…I wasn't referring to your…to anything…"

"You know you're talking out loud right now, right?"

"Oh, shut up. Ox."

"Nag."

She glared at him and Oz gave her his innocent "what?" face.

"Let me get this straight…there are people out there so rich that they can't even bother to shop for themselves? They have to actually hire people to *shop* for them?"

"No. It's not like that at all," she said, glaring at him.

"It's exactly like that. You shop for a living. For people too lazy to shop for themselves."

"No. You've misunderstood. I offer a valuable service for people who need advice."

"Really? Like what?"

"Like…okay. For instance, I had a lady come in a couple months ago. She'd gotten her first office job and needed a new wardrobe to go with it. I had already helped her pick out her initial interview outfit and then we worked on stocking her closet with everything she'd need once she got the job. We set her up completely. Those are the clients I really love. I do have a few on the freelance side who are what you'd call frivolous, but I think they're fun. Like the ones who need furniture or some exotic birthday gift or something. I don't get too many of those in North Carolina, though."

Oz shrugged. "Well, it still sounds hokey to me, but if that's what you want to do with your life…"

"I didn't say it's what I wanted to do with my life. But I don't want to sit around doing nothing, either, and I'm good at it."

"I don't doubt that," he muttered, hurrying on before she could give voice to the outrage on her face. "So what does your family think?"

She turned her gaze back to the rain drenched trees that seemed to be flying by. "I told you what they all do. I'm sure you can imagine."

"It can't be that bad."

"Every member of my family is at the top of their field. Every one of them. Except me."

"Ah, come on. Don't sell yourself short. I bet you are a

world-class shopper."

She rolled her eyes and folded her arms across her chest. "And you wonder why I don't want to talk to you."

Oz grinned, having a lot more fun than he probably should be, considering the topic of conversation.

"Yeah, okay, I get that it sucks to not live up to your family's expectations, but come on. It's not like you're slinging newspapers in the middle of the night."

Cherice snorted. "No. I haven't sunk that low yet. But I might as well have in my family's eyes."

Oz's grip tightened on the steering wheel. He wasn't sure what had made him use newspapers as an example. It's not like he didn't already know how she'd feel about that. And he wasn't ashamed of what he did. He made good money with his route. Enough to pay several bills. And it was honest work that he could do at night that didn't mess with his other jobs. Still, it stung to hear her dismiss it so harshly.

"So why do you care what they think? It sounds like you only aimed for med school to please your family. Did you even want to go?"

"Of course. Being a physician is an honorable profession," she said, her voice completely monotone like she was repeating something she'd memorized from birth.

Oz snorted. "Yeah. Say that a few more times and I might actually believe you."

Cher's full lips twisted into a petulant pout. "I'm not trying to convince you of anything. It's my life. I don't know why you care so much, anyway."

Oz's hands tightened on the steering wheel with the effort to hold on to his temper. "Because you've got everything and you're sitting there all depressed, acting like you've got no options. I mean, come on! You've probably got more money than most people will see in a lifetime. You don't have to worry about bills or keeping a roof over your head or food on your table. You could go anywhere, do anything you want. So why don't you?"

"That is so typical!" Her mouth snapped shut and she dragged a deep breath in through her nose. When she spoke again, her voice was a bit calmer, but her face was still flushed. "Just because my family has money, people always think my life is so easy. You would never understand the kind of pressure I'm under all the time. You have no idea what it's like to be the only one in your family who has failed at becoming their ideal offspring. To be the only one who hasn't done anything to build up the family name. I'd give up every dime they've ever given me to have the freedom you have, to do what I really want to do."

His jaw clenched. Only people who had never been without money talked so causally about throwing it all away. She might think she really meant it, but she didn't know what it felt like to worry about whether or not you could pay the rent that month. She'd never had to function on three hours of sleep because she'd spent every waking second working whatever jobs she could find to keep food on the table. Despite what she obviously believed, someone like her would never understand what it felt like to want something with all your heart and not be able to go for it.

He kept his gaze glued to the road. "That's just the thing, Cher. You *do* have the freedom to do what you really want to do. Yeah, your family might be disappointed in you. They might even be pissed as hell. But they won't really be hurt by it. They won't lose anything that really matters."

She looked back out the window at the overcast skies. "You don't get it."

"No. I don't. And neither do you. I don't have any freedom. I do what I have to do to take care of my family. I gave up my dreams a long time ago so I could do something more important. There was a good reason for me to do what I did. But it wasn't really a choice. If I didn't do what I do, my family would be starving on the streets. That's not the case with you. There's just no good reason for you to do it."

"Just because it's not a good reason to you doesn't mean it isn't one to me," she said, plucking at the hem of her shirt again.

Damn. She had him there. He still disagreed with her. She was being ridiculous letting her family dictate how she lived her life. His family did the same to a certain extent, he supposed. But because they needed him. Not because they had some screwed up priorities about what really mattered.

"Touché," he said with a small smile.

"You know, we really aren't so different. We're both just regular people, wanting to make our families happy." Her lips echoed his smile.

He completely disagreed on the whole "regular people" bit. There was nothing regular about her. She'd break out in hives if she had to be around regular people for more than two minutes. But he didn't feel like ruining the tenuous, and probably temporary, peace in the car to point that out. At least not with that line of discussion.

He needed to change the subject. "I'm hungry. Let's find someplace to eat."

A few miles down the road, they passed an exit sign with a bunch of symbols for food joints. He pointed to it. "Any preference?"

She grimaced. "Isn't there any place where we can get something that doesn't come with a plastic toy?"

Oz spied a place just off the road and turned his head so she wouldn't see his smile. She thought she was regular, *hmm*? Let's see how she did around real *regular* folk.

"Looks like there's a place down the street a ways."

"Anything is fine with me."

Yeah. They'd just see about that. He pulled into the parking lot of the Roadkill Roadhouse and shut off the car.

"What are we doing here?" Cherice asked, looking out the window with a frown.

"We're getting something to eat. You said you wanted something that came without plastic toys. They've probably got waitresses and everything."

She didn't look convinced.

"Come on, Cher. You might be able to live off granola bars and water but I need something a little more substantial than rabbit food."

"And this is the best place you thought we could find?"

For food? Hell no, not by a long shot. But it would serve his other purposes just fine.

"It'll do. Come on, I'm melting out here. It's gotta be air conditioned, at least."

"So's the car," she muttered.

She climbed out and glanced down at herself. His shirt hung halfway down her thighs and was big enough for two of her, and the flip flops...he didn't bother hiding his grin when he caught sight of her toes, painted red with black and white dots which made each nail look like a ladybug sitting on her toes. Surprisingly playful. She could have easily put both feet in one flip flop but at least they provided some protection.

Oz held the door open for her and tried not to smile as he looked around the run-down diner. He couldn't have picked a better place to make her squirm than if he'd spent a month researching locations. It would do perfectly to prove to the princess, once and for all, that he was right. They were from two different worlds and she could spout that *we're the same regular people wanting the same things* nonsense all she wanted. People like her were nothing like people like him, and her attempts to say otherwise weren't fooling him at all.

Her repeated comments against, for the lack of a better phrase, his social class, made his butt pucker and he was in the mood to yank her chain a little. The fact she didn't even realize how insulting she was made it even worse. So. A little harmless revenge might be just the ticket to improve his mood a bit. Let's see how she did in a real dive.

He slid into a booth near the window so he could keep an eye on the car. The fact he felt the need to do that probably pointed to the diner being a little more of a dive than even he was comfortable with. But there was no backing out now, though it was a bit of a moot point since he couldn't really see through the grime on the glass, anyway.

He picked up the menu and looked over his options. He'd made it through the appetizers before he realized Cherice was standing at the end of the table staring at him.

He sighed. "Cher, sit. I realize it's not Spago or wherever the hell you usually eat, but it's not going to kill you."

"It might." She glared at him but slid carefully into the booth. He pushed a menu across the table to her but she left it where it was and opened her handbag, taking out the travel wet-wipes.

"What are you doing?" he asked.

Her eyes narrowed even farther. "I don't feel like eating my meal on top of whatever this substance is," she said, scrubbing at the table in front of her.

Oz ducked back behind his menu. He did enjoy watching her being uncomfortable after spending the last several hours with her. But even he had to admit the place was nasty. Fifty-year-old wallpaper peeled from the walls in spots and the broken neon light outside the dirty window was probably going to induce a seizure in someone at any minute. An old jukebox in the corner didn't look like it had been touched in years and Oz was pretty sure the woman standing outside who had just spit on her cigarette and tucked it behind her ear was their waitress.

She nodded at him through the window and shouted, "Be right with you!"

Oz didn't dare look at Cher. He could feel her look of disgust through the laminated menu he held.

Their waitress came back inside and dug a pad and pencil out of her apron. After noisily hacking into the crook of her arm, she asked, "You folks ready?"

Oz put down the menu. "I'll have the tuna melt and fries, and a large Coke, please."

"*Um hmm*. And you?" She turned to Cher who hadn't even opened her menu.

"*Um*. Just a salad with ranch dressing, please. And a bottled water if you have one."

"Sure thing."

The moment the waitress lumbered away, Cher lit into

him. "If I get food poisoning from this place I'm aiming at you."

"Oh please. I'm sure the food is fine. Even places like this have to follow the health code. Besides, it's usually these kinds of places that have the best food. Like hidden local treasures."

Cher shook her head. "Impressive."

"What?"

"You almost sound like you believe that."

"I do."

"*Uh huh.*"

Oz managed to keep up the act until their waitress came back with their meals. She seemed to have forgotten their drinks entirely but one look at their food and Oz had no intention of reminding her.

"*Bon appétit,*" she said, in a surprisingly good French accent.

Cher looked at her salad and then looked back at him. He peered into her bowl. The lettuce looked as though it had been microwaved. And he hoped that dressing was blue cheese because if not…he swallowed and turned his attention to his own plate. And…he wished he hadn't. Was tuna supposed to be gray?

"Go ahead," Cher said, a little smile dancing on her lips. "I dare you."

Oz narrowed his eyes. Oh, she was not going to win this one. He picked up one of the pieces of toast covered in what he assumed was tuna smothered in a layer of what looked like a melted crayon but must have been the cheese.

He brought it to his mouth. Got a good whiff of it. And put it right back down. Even his pride wasn't worth the near-certain food-poisoning episode that was sitting on his plate.

"Fine," he said, standing up and slapping a twenty on the table. "You win. Let's go."

Cher gathered up her bag, a huge grin spreading across her face. Oz stopped short. He'd never seen her smile so genuinely. It transformed her. She was already beautiful, in an impersonal way, kind of like the china dolls his sister used to collect as a child.

But that smile…it warmed her from the inside out, softened her features, made her seem happy and carefree. Now that right there, *that* person he could like. He could more than like. Before he could get too excited over her, Cher pushed through the doors and the humid heat slapped him in the face like a wet blanket.

He hurried to get back in the car and crank the air conditioning up.

"Well, that was fun," Cher said.

"Okay, sorry. I didn't think it would be quite that bad."

"*Uh huh.* Well I have no intention of getting out of this car again in this getup so do you have any other bright ideas?"

Oz couldn't really blame her. "Actually," he said, remembering the sign they'd passed not too far back. "I do have an idea."

Cher sighed. "Fine. Just wake me up when we get there."

She leaned her head back and closed her eyes, laying one arm over them. Oz snorted. That pose couldn't say "prima donna" any more than if she'd had it tattooed across her forehead.

She kept her eyes closed, like she was afraid to see what new hellhole he was going to drag her to. He couldn't blame her, he supposed, after what he'd just subjected her to.

He pulled into a parking lot and stopped the car.

Cherice peeked out from under her arm. "Where are we now?"

"Sonic."

"What?" She leaned forward to look out the windshield, a small frown creasing her forehead.

"You've never been to a Sonic?"

She shook her head.

"Well, I'm glad your first time gets to be with me."

Her gaze shot to his and he fought to keep his expression bland. Just innocent ol' Oz, clueless as to what his harmless statements might imply. Her eyes narrowed, not buying it for a second.

He gestured to the menu. "Great food, amazing ice cream, and you don't even have to get out of your car. They'll bring your food right to you."

"Really? Okay...I can get behind that."

Oz laughed. "Just pick what you want from the menu."

She nearly leaned across his lap to see the menu items and he froze. "Sorry," she murmured. "I don't have my reading glasses."

He would have thought she was playing with him, but she seemed genuinely embarrassed to be half in his lap. And she *was* squinting at the menu board.

"No problem," he said, his words sounding slightly choked. He cleared his throat and took a deep breath. A faint hint of some exotic flower filled his senses and it was all he could do not to hold her close so he could breathe her in.

She sat back a little, a slight frown narrowing her eyes, and looked like she was about to say something. But before she could, a loud noise from the direction of her stomach interrupted. It reminded him that his own stomach was about ready to turn itself inside out in a fit of hunger. So he did his best to ignore the woman in his lap and concentrate on the menu.

"Okay," she said, "don't judge, but I'll have that hamburger meal there with the curly fries and a cookies-and-cream blast thing."

"Are you kidding? Total girl after my own heart," he said with a wink. "I think I'll have the exact same thing."

Her cheeks flushed and her frown deepened. Like she was attracted to him but really hated it. Not surprising. He supposed he wasn't the type of guy she was brought up to be attracted to. He might ring all her bells but he wasn't the one who was supposed to be pulling the ropes. Too bad for her.

He ordered and then leaned against his door, letting one finger stroke along his upper lip while he stared at her. Her eyes followed his finger, her lips parting slightly, and he couldn't keep the smug look from his face. It must chap her ass something fierce to be turned on by him. Only he really didn't have room to judge her so harshly because the sight of the tongue that quickly darted out to moisten her lips made things clench low in his belly.

Time to shake things up before he took his chances and found out what would happen if he kissed those lips of hers.

"So, what is it you really want to do?" he asked.

She threw her hands up like some 1950s movie starlet throwing a hissy fit. Damn, but it was fun to aggravate her.

"You don't give up, do you?" she asked.

Oz grinned. "No. So you might as well just answer. I can do this all day. And you can't escape. It's starting to rain again," he said, pointing out the window where a few fat raindrops lazily ran down the glass.

"What difference does it make?"

"I want to know."

She looked out the window, her finger tracing little circles on her leg. "I don't have it pinned down yet. But I'd like to be…I don't know, like a life coach, maybe."

She couldn't have surprised him more if she'd announced she wanted to be a headliner at some strip club. In fact, *that* he might have actually understood. She'd make good money and piss her parents off. Win-win. But a life coach? Her?

"A life coach?"

"Yes," she said, though she frowned a bit. "Or…maybe start my own company that expands on what I'm already doing. It could be the whole package."

"Shopping and life coaching?"

She sighed like he was totally missing the point and she didn't want to explain it to him for the thousandth time. "It's not shopping."

"So, clothes and advice?"

"Something like that."

She glanced over at him, and despite the fact that he wanted to throttle her ninety percent of their time together, the look on her face made his heart twist. He'd found a puppy once that had been abused. It had been huddled in a ball, drawn in on itself, its eyes full of fear and pain when he'd first reached out to it. Cher had that same look in her eyes; like she expected him to kick her, and she just wanted to hide.

"No wise cracks?"

Oz shook his head and swallowed past the sudden

tightness in his throat. "No. I think that's great."

"Really?"

"Yeah. A little odd maybe," he said, winking at her. "But great."

Cher smiled and a little of the ache in Oz's chest eased. He might not think she was qualified for the job, but at least it seemed geared toward helping people, in some weird way. Maybe there was a real person under all that glitz and glamour.

"So, why don't you be a life coach or start up your business, then?"

"I've looked into it. And I do volunteer."

"No, I mean for real. Quit shopping. Go do your thing."

She shook her head. "My parents don't think it is a good use of my time."

"And being a personal shopper is?"

Cher snorted. "No. And I've told you, that's not really what I do. But I think the only reason they've left me alone until now is because they haven't figured out what to do with me yet. Opening a business, or being a life coach? I'd have to go to school, get certified, and spend a ton of money to get everything I need to run the type of operation I'm thinking of running. It's a major undertaking. A career. One that would be completely unacceptable for them. There is no advantage for me or the family that they'd understand."

"But it would be advantageous, to you. You've got to start living your own life at some point. So go do it."

"Oh sure. I'll just go home and interrupt my sister's wedding to tell my parents that to make up for completely failing at everything else they wanted for me, I'm going to dedicate my life to continuing what I'm doing, only on a much larger scale. That'll go over real well. I'm sure my sister will appreciate the knock-down drag-out fight in the middle of her wedding."

"Why not? You have the right to do what you want with your life, don't you? Do it. I dare you."

"Good plan. I'll just go destroy my life on a dare."

"Don't they want you to be happy?"

Cher looked down at her lap, her nose wrinkling in a delicate sneer. "Not nearly as much as they want to preserve and glorify the name of Debusshere."

Oz shook his head. "Sorry, I just have a hard time believing any parent would rather their kid be miserable her whole life than go against some grand plan for the betterment of the family."

"Yeah, well like I said, you wouldn't understand. My family has had our whole lives planned out since before we were born. What schools we would go to, what friends we'd have. We were on a preschool waiting list when we were still in the womb. You have no idea what it's like to have the kind of pressure on you that I do. When you come from a family like mine, what you do matters."

Oz snorted, any lingering amusement or sympathy for her gone. "So, apparently when you're just a poor second-class citizen like I am, living paycheck to tiny paycheck, what you do with your life doesn't matter."

Cher's mouth dropped open. "No. That's not what I meant, at all."

Yeah. That's what was so sad about it. She obviously didn't see anything wrong with what she'd just said. It didn't even occur to her that it might be just the slightest bit offensive.

"Well, Cher, no matter what you think, when you're ready to live your own life, all you really have to do is go for it. I guess we'll see if you ever have the balls to do it."

Her eyes narrowed. "Since I do not have *balls*, I guess you'll be waiting a long time. And will you please stop calling me Cher. My name is Cherice."

"Fine. Sorry. Cherice."

"Thank you, Nathaniel."

"Oz."

Cher just groaned.

His eyes twinkled in amusement and that insanely kiss-able mouth pulled into that sexy little half grin. Cherice's heart did that inappropriate flutter again, which kicked up a hundred notches at the thought of her lying in his lap a few moments earlier. His firm, warm, very appealing lap. She sat back with a slight frown, but her cheeks were uncomfortably warm. What was wrong with her? She should not be reacting to him like that. And what the hell was he doing throwing around winks and half stripping in front of her and rubbing that lip and…and…*sniffing* her?

She had half a mind to…*oohhh the food is being brought right to our car!* How had she never been to one of these places before?

Nathaniel handed her order to her. She eyed the huge pile of food, knowing she should probably be a good girl and eat her meal first. "Screw it," she muttered, scooping a huge spoonful of ice cream into her mouth. "Oh my God, this should be illegal."

Nathaniel's eyebrows rose. She didn't even care. She'd barely eaten anything all day and she hadn't had anything so sinful in months. Or longer. She shoved another spoonful in, swallowed it down, and then grabbed the bridge of her nose and groaned.

"Ow. Brain freeze."

Nathaniel burst out laughing. "Slow down there, Cher. We've got plenty of time."

"Cherice," she mumbled around another scoop-full of ice cream.

"Try dipping the fries into it."

She grimaced. Nathaniel just laughed and bit into his own burger. "I swear it's good. Try it."

She held out a fry and the shake. "You first."

"My pleasure." He grabbed the fry, loaded it with ice cream, and popped it in his mouth. "Delicious," he said, licking his fingers.

Cherice licked her own suddenly dry lips, her gaze glued to his. It did look delicious. The ice cream. The ice cream looked delicious.

She realized he was staring at her staring at him and jerked back. He grinned, took a fry and dunked it in her shake, holding it out to her.

"Come on."

She leaned forward, keeping her gaze glued to his. The salty, sweet deliciousness of the ice-cream-smothered fry was a surprise.

"It's good," she mumbled around the food.

"Told you." He smiled and licked the finger that had just been holding the fry. "Eat up. We gotta get back on the road. We've still got about six-and-a half hours before we get to your parents' place."

Cherice put another fry in her mouth, barely tasting the food. All her attention was riveted on the finger sliding in and out of Nathaniel's mouth. Her stomach flipped while the rest of her body tightened as if waiting for him to drag that finger along her skin.

What the hell was she thinking? She ripped her gaze from him and focused on her food, though her appetite had taken a nose dive. She decided it was the result of inhaling greasy fries smothered in ice cream and had nothing at all to do with the massive guilt trip she was riding for lusting after the finger-licking married man sitting next to her.

They tossed their trash and got back on the road. It didn't last long, though.

"The West Virginia Welcome Center is a few miles up the road. Picture time," he said, grinning.

Cherice groaned, but inwardly she still thought it was pretty cute that he was taking the pictures for his son. She would have preferred they had a little nicer weather for it, but she really couldn't complain too much since he was the one running out to stand in the rain under the signs. She hoped the signs for Maryland and Pennsylvania were the ones that hung over the freeway or they'd be stopping every ten minutes. They didn't have much of Maryland to go through.

Nathaniel pulled into the Welcome Center lot and parked the car. Thankfully, the rain had let up for a few minutes. Of course, that meant the humidity was off-the-charts stifling. But she'd at least be able to take his picture without both of them getting soaked.

Looked like they'd need to wait their turn for the sign, though. An elderly couple was attempting to take a selfie of the two of them in front of it. Cherice smiled and stepped forward.

"Would you like me to take a picture of the two of you?" she asked, holding out her hand for their camera.

"Oh, that would be wonderful, thank you," the woman said. "Would you mind taking a few?"

"Not at all." She smiled at them and glanced at Nathaniel. He smiled at her, but it was more of a thoughtful expression than amused.

Cherice snapped several pictures of the couple. They were just downright freaking adorable. Married forty-five years and still looked as in love as they must have the day they married.

"Your turn!" the woman said after Cherice handed her back her camera.

"Oh, no that's all right," Cherice said. "We were just going to take his picture."

"Oh that's silly. Come on, both of you."

The woman herded Nathaniel and Cherice together in front of the sign, deftly plucking Nathaniel's phone out of his hand.

"Now, put your arm around her, young man. Don't be shy!"

Nathaniel just laughed and did as he was told. Cherice bit back another argument. The woman didn't seem like she'd take no for an answer, so it was probably just easier to go along with it and get it over with. Though standing there with Nathaniel's arms wrapped around her was making her react in ways she really shouldn't be reacting to a married man. She shouldn't be thinking about how warm his hand felt against the small of her back. Or of how strong his arms felt around her. Or wondering if his lips felt as soft and full as they looked. Or if that faint musk scent was cologne or soap or just *him*. Nope. Shouldn't be thinking any of those things.

The woman snapped several pictures and then handed the phone back to Nathaniel with a smile.

"You two make a lovely couple. I hope you have as many years together as my Frank and I have had."

Cherice shook her head, her stomach bottoming out. "No, we're—"

Nathaniel wrapped his arm around her waist and pulled her against him, cutting off her attempt to set the woman straight.

"Thank you, ma'am, that's very kind of you. You two travel safe now."

Cherice stayed stiffly in his arms while they walked back to the car and he opened her door for her. But the second he got in the car, Nathaniel cut her off before she could get the words out.

"It was a whole lot easier to go along with it than waste a bunch of time explaining that we're just strangers on a road trip together. Sorry if it embarrassed you that they thought we were together."

He started the car and paid a lot of careful attention to getting out of the parking lot and back on the road. He didn't look at her once.

"No, that's not why…"

"It doesn't matter. Mind if I turn the radio on?"

He hit the power button and cranked it up before she could answer.

Cherice sat back in her seat, frowning. What the hell had just happened?

Chapter Seven

His overreaction at the Welcome Center had almost gotten to Oz enough that he wanted to apologize for snapping at Cher. Her instant denial when the old lady had assumed they were a couple had stung his pride.

But at the end of the day, it didn't matter if she was ashamed of him or not. They weren't a couple and never would be. Six more hours and they'd probably never lay eyes on each other again, so what difference did it make what her opinion of him was? Either way, he didn't feel like spending the next few hours ignoring each other.

And then she opened her mouth again.

"Do you think there are any places to get some clothes out here? These are totally ruined. It doesn't have to be anywhere nice or anything. Just wherever you'd usually go would be fine."

Oz grunted. "Do you even hear the words coming out of your mouth?"

She raised a startled gaze to his. "What did I say?"

He just shook his head. "Never mind. Don't you do enough shopping for your day job? The stores might like a break. I thought we were in a hurry."

She scowled at him. "I can still smell the ketchup, which is mixing with the baby-powder smell from the wipes and giving me a headache. And making me nauseous, which isn't really a great idea in a small car on a long trip. Not to mention the fact that my pants have a mud stain halfway up one leg and I'm wearing plastic shoes fifty sizes too big. There is no way I'm walking into my parents' house looking like this."

Okay, the ketchup remains were giving him a bit of a headache too, not that he'd admit it. Which was a shame because the nasty vinegar smell obscured the soft jasmine scent of her hair he'd gotten a whiff of when she'd practically crawled in his lap to see the menu. It was too bad she was such a pill. Because she was kind of adorable when she wasn't being a total twit.

"There's not a whole lot of options around here. Nothing you'd approve of, I'm sure."

"I'm not asking for Bloomingdale's. I just want something clean and dry that hopefully fits. And if I'm lucky maybe something without any offensive, egotistical catch phrases involving meat euphemisms. Surely that's a possibility."

Oz shook his head with a wry smile, about to tell her she'd have to just suffer, hopefully in silence, until he saw the sign off the highway. He signaled to get over and took the next exit.

"Well, Cher, you're in luck." He made a left and nodded at the looming superstore as it came into view. "You should be able to find anything you need there."

Cher looked out the windshield and Oz grinned at the small frown creasing her brow. He could no more picture Cherice Buchanan Debusshere prancing around the aisles of a supersized one-stop-shop discount mart than he could picture himself duded up in a fancy tux at some fundraiser event her type always frequented.

"Don't worry. I'm sure you can find something there that won't make you break out in hives."

Cher's scowl deepened. "The only thing that's going to make me break out in hives is you."

Oz shrugged. "Don't blame me if you burst into flames the moment you step inside."

He pulled into the parking lot and found a spot right up front. Apparently, they were the only idiots out and about on a day like today as he was stuck chauffeuring a spoiled snot who was determined to keep him in his place. He hadn't missed the look in her eyes with the whole fry episode earlier. She'd liked the little show he'd put on. And then she'd had to go and open that mouth of hers. Hypocrite.

"Watch out for the puddle," he muttered, hopping across the massive pond that covered half the parking lot. It wasn't all that wide, but his long legs had barely made the distance. It was long enough she'd probably need to walk around it.

She took a couple tentative steps, trying to tiptoe her way through it. Not the easiest thing to do when her oversized flip flops kept slapping the water with each step, splashing water up the back of her legs.

He folded his arms and watched as she took one tiny step after another. "Any day now."

"You could help here." She held out her hands, her purse

dangling from one arm.

"Oh, right, sorry." Oz leaned over, took her purse from her arm, then turned back toward the store, ignoring her outraged gasp.

He waited by the door, watching her prance and splash across the rest of the puddle. He'd never been so purposely rude to anyone, let alone a woman, in his life. But he couldn't deny the intense streak of satisfaction that came from watching the woman struggle a little. She'd been a pain in his ass all day.

She'd just made it to the other side when one foot stepped on the back end of the other flip flop. She landed with a wet thud right on her pampered derriere. Water sprayed everywhere.

Oz's heart twisted for a split second but the growl and muttered curses she was letting fly indicated only that she was pissed off. No sign of pain. She was fine.

"Seriously? Are you just going to stand there and watch me?"

"Oh," Oz said, reaching her in two long strides. "My apologies."

He reached down. And handed her purse back to her. "There you go." He turned to walk away again.

"Nathaniel!"

"Oz."

"Oh my God!"

"You don't have to call me God. Oz will do."

She swished her hand through the puddle, spraying him with the murky water. He gasped and jumped back, wiping his face. Okay. Maybe he deserved that one.

Cher hauled herself off the ground and stalked past him

to the door. He decided to throw her a bone and held the door open with a polite grin and a little bow. She stomped past him, flicking her wet ponytail in his direction. It caught him in the face with a wet slap. He wiped his cheek. Okay, he deserved that, too.

"All right, get what you need, but let's make it quick," Oz said, frowning when she grabbed a cart and headed straight for the women's section. "The day isn't getting any longer. I'd like to get as far as we can before it gets too dark."

She waved at him over her shoulder and disappeared into a pile of clearance racks. If he hadn't known better, he'd have sworn she belonged there. He watched in amazement as she tore into a stack of shirts like she was a hyena feasting on a rhino. He shook his head and left her to it.

He took his time wandering around the store, ending up in the travel supply section. He grabbed another pack of wet wipes and a container of aspirin. Knowing Cherice, they'd need both. And soon.

Oz found her near the fitting rooms talking to a woman who looked like the proverbial soccer mom. Cher was holding up a dress in front of the woman, her face more animated than he'd ever seen it. The woman laughed and went back to the dressing rooms. Oz started forward again but stopped when a teenage girl came out dressed in a God-awful pantsuit. He expected Cher to wrinkle her pampered little nose up but she tilted her head and rubbed her finger across her lips like she was thinking.

"It's not bad. I think something a little more fitted might work better. Here, let's try these," she said, handing the girl a pair of slacks and a blouse, "and see how these look with them." She added a shoe box and a necklace to the pile.

Oz crossed his arms and leaned against a wall of shelves holding jeans. What was Cher up to?

The girl beamed at Cher and hurried back to the room just as the woman Oz assumed was her mother, going by their hair color and features, came back out in a little black dress that showed off her great legs.

Cher clapped. "That one is perfect!"

The woman smiled and did a little spin. "It is, isn't it?" She leaned over and pulled Cher into a hug. "Thanks so much for your help. I thought black was too depressing for a party but…"

Cher laughed. "You can say it, Annie. You look *hot*."

The woman, Annie, laughed with her but the girl came back out before she could say anything else. Annie clasped her hands to her chest and aimed one of those proud motherly looks at her daughter.

She did look much better. The black slacks fit her perfectly and the pale pink blouse and black Mary Janes were youthful enough she didn't look like a little girl playing dress-up but professional enough that she would fit in at any office.

"Oh honey," Annie said, "you look great! You're going to get that job for sure."

The girl smiled and smoothed her hands down the legs of the slacks. "Can I get it?"

"Of course. Let's go get changed and then hit the salon."

The girl grinned and they headed back to the dressing room.

Cher looked up and saw Oz. The smile she aimed at him damn near stopped his heart for a second. What the hell? He couldn't help but smile back. The happiness on her face was contagious.

He pushed away from his wall and came to stand beside her. He glanced down in her cart and his jaw dropped. Her cart was filled with a couple of frilly dresses, yoga pants, a few silky bits that put images in his mind that he couldn't block no matter how hard he tried, and a long slinky bit of silk that must have been a nightgown. There were also shoe boxes, and one of those little shoe hanger thingies holding a much more feminine and appropriate-sized pair of flip flops.

"I was gone fifteen minutes. Tops," he said.

"I know. What took you so long?"

His mouth opened and shut. If there was an Olympic event for shopping, she'd have the gold. Hands down.

The mother and daughter came back out of the dressing room and gave Cher a happy wave. "Thanks for all your help!"

"My pleasure. Have fun at your reunion and good luck with your job interview, Katy."

They waved again and headed off. Oz looked down at Cher, his eyebrows raised in question. "Friends of yours?"

"Just some nice people I ran into over in the dress section. They have everything in this store!" she said with a genuine smile. "I could spend all day here."

Oz found himself returning it with a grin of his own.

"I bet you could. Unfortunately, we need to get back on the road. Let's check out and get out of here."

"Not so fast," she said, grabbing his arm.

"What?"

"Follow me. You need a few things too."

"No, I don't."

She pulled him into the men's department over to a

display of men's slacks.

"Yes, you do. You have a job interview tomorrow."

"I know. I have clothes for that."

She bit her flip, frowning.

"What?" he asked.

"Okay, don't take this the wrong way, but I got a peek at your interview outfit when we were at the gas station and you were digging that wonderful article of clothing out of your suitcase," she said, gesturing to his shirt.

"Yeah. And?"

"It's nice. It's just…probably not what a New York company is used to people wearing to interviews."

He shrugged. She was cringing a little, like she expected him to lash out or be embarrassed. Really, it was more curiosity than anything else that had him asking, "So what would they be expecting?"

Cher smiled, relief flooding her face, and grabbed a pair of slacks off the rack. She took them off the hanger, holding them up to him. He took a step back.

"Oh, knock it off and bring your stubborn ass back here."

Both eyebrows rose.

"Look, you want to impress these people, right?"

Oz nodded, afraid to contradict her while she was holding a blunt object, aka the hanger, so close to his favorite body parts.

"Well then, it wouldn't hurt you to jazz things up a bit."

Oz straightened, his body going rigid in a knee-jerk reaction to the probably unintentional meaning behind her words. If he wanted to make a good impression, he *was* going to have to play dress-up and pretend he could hob knob with his "betters." He'd already known that, so he knew he was being overly sensitive. In fact, if he could have gone out and bought a new suit, he would have. He agreed with everything she was saying.

But it stung coming out of her mouth.

"Here," she said, loading his arms with an assortment of slacks, shirts, ties, and something he thought might be a sweater-vest.

He held it up. "Really?"

"Okay, maybe not that." She took it back and tossed it on the table. "Go try on the rest."

He let out a long, suffering sigh but did as Her Highness commanded. And damn, but her choices were pretty decent. More than decent. He looked good. In clothes he never would have chosen for himself. Maybe she was on to something with her whole personal shopper idea. She'd chosen something really great for that girl, too. If that's what she really did for a living, it somehow seemed a little less frivolous after seeing the smile light up that girl's face. Cher had made her happy, had really helped her. Maybe that should be something he applauded instead of mocking.

Thirty seconds after he tugged the first shirt on, she called impatiently from the waiting area. "Let me see!"

"What?"

"Come out so I can see?"

"What am I, five?"

"Oh, be quiet and come out here."

He chuckled. She drove him nuts but she was fun to rile up.

"Nathaniel?"

"Oz!"

She groaned and he laughed harder.

"All right, keep your shirt on, I'll be right out."

A sudden image of Cher slowly removing her shirt hit him like a fist to the gut and he shook his head to dislodge it. But he couldn't help wondering what a woman who was so determined to be in control of everything would be like if she were driven so crazy she lost all control. Then again, she didn't seem to *have* any control over her own life. That belonged to her family. Maybe that's what made her fight so hard for control of everything else. She was a walking contradiction in more ways than one. If he tried to figure her out he'd probably have an aneurysm.

"Nathaniel!"

"Oh, my God woman, hang on!"

He finished getting the tie on and took a good look at himself in the mirror. He'd tried on a few different options, but this was his favorite, by far. Surprising, actually. He stepped out of the dressing room and walked toward Cher.

She straightened from where she'd been leaning against a counter holding watches, her mouth dropping open momentarily before she snapped it shut again.

Heh. The lady must like what she sees. Oz stood a bit straighter, his thumbs trailing along the waist of the close-fitting, charcoal slacks, making sure the lavender shirt was tucked in all the way. Cher's eyes followed every movement of his hands. Interesting.

He ran his hand down the dark purple tie to flatten it against his chest, plastering the material to what he knew were a great set of defined abs. Lavender and purple. Not colors he'd ever in a million years be caught dead in. Colors? Was it two different colors or did it count as different types of the same color? Ah hell, he didn't know. But he had to give it to her, it looked great, judging by the sudden heat in her eyes.

That heat…it triggered an answering burning in him. It also scared the hell out of him. They had no call feeling anything for each other but grudging tolerance. Nothing good could come of *heat*. Besides, if he was seeing what he thought he was seeing it was only because he was all dressed up and fancy like one of her pretty New York boys. And that just wasn't the real him.

It was also just as likely she wasn't feeling anything at all and at that very moment was just trying to figure out why he was staring at her like a dog in the deli case and the look in her eyes was fear he'd suddenly gone completely daft. Which apparently he had.

"I think that's the one," she said, her husky voice breaking the tense silence.

He blinked and forced a smile. "You think so?"

"They won't be able to resist you in that." The words were so quiet he barely caught what she'd said. Oh, but he'd heard it. He took a step toward her and she took one back.

Neither one moved again, both frozen in a weird staring contest. Oz wasn't quite sure what would happen if he let her win. He took one more step toward her and she blinked, dropping her gaze.

"We better get moving if we want to make New York by midnight."

Oz nodded, the weird spell between them broken. He stepped back into the dressing room, not sure he wanted to try and analyze what had just happened. It was probably nothing, anyway. He'd just been stunned by the fact that Cher hadn't been shooting some hideously offensive sentiment out of her mouth. The fact that he was lying to himself wasn't a possibility he was ready to accept. Yet.

"Nathaniel?"

The sound of her voice right outside the dressing room made him jump.

"What are you doing in here?"

"Toss me your clothes."

He laughed, low and deep. "If you want my clothes, why don't you come in here and get them?"

"Nathaniel!"

He grinned. He knew what she meant, but she walked right into that one.

"I just thought I'd go get in line while you're getting dressed."

"You can't wait another two minutes?"

Her exasperated sigh filtered through the door and he grinned. "All right, fine."

If she wanted his clothes, he'd give them to her. He opened the door and tossed her his tie. "Here."

Then he started unbuttoning his shirt. Her eyes flew open, her jaw dropping. She didn't say a word, just watched as he finished unbuttoning and shrugged out of the shirt. Her gaze remained riveted to his bare chest and he wondered just how long she'd stand there staring. She'd surprised him making it as long as she had. He thought for sure she'd freak out by the second button.

All right, then. His hands dropped to the button of his pants. That finally jolted her out of her daze.

"What are you doing?" she gasped and turned around.

He smiled and closed the door, quickly stripping the pants and tossing them over the door.

"There. I'll be out in a few."

"I'll...*um*, I'll meet you up front."

"Yeah, yeah."

He took his time getting dressed. That strip tease might not have been the wisest course of action. Her reaction had certainly bitten him in the ass. So to speak. The problem was, he hadn't expected her to *have* a reaction. A little outrage maybe, some uncomfortable squirming, sure. That open-mouthed, heated, hungry stare that suggested she very much wanted him to keep going? No. *That*, he wasn't expecting.

He took a few deeps breaths, concentrating on safe, non-sexual thoughts until all body parts had returned to their non-full, non-upright positions. They needed to get a move on. He tugged his clothes on and hurried to the front of the store.

But, when he got to the registers, Cher had already checked out and was waiting near the restrooms, bags in hand. And wearing one of her outfits. A red sundress with little white polka dots that matched her toes, or would if they were visible. At the moment, they were hidden by a pair of bright yellow rain boots that stretched to her knees.

A clear plastic poncho covered the entire ensemble, even her hair, which she'd taken out of the pony tail. It was now half swept up with some sort of plastic doo-dad. A bright yellow umbrella dangled from her hand. The tag proclaimed it "a smile for when the skies were gray." He snorted. The damn thing must have a giant smiley face on it. She looked...absolutely adorable. Like a regular girl on her way to a picnic. Only he knew she was anything but regular.

"What's with the getup?"

"It's pouring again. Can't you hear it?"

He frowned, listening for a moment. Then he realized that dull roar he hadn't really acknowledged was the sound of rain hitting the roof of the giant store.

She held out her foot and shook it around a bit. "No more wet feet."

"I see that." He grinned and gestured at her outfit. "Very nice."

She took the compliment, even if his tone was a bit grudging, and graced him with another one of those smiles that made the sun come out and warm him through and through.

"Thank you."

He nodded, a bit knocked off guard, and glanced around, expecting his pile of stuff to be waiting on a conveyor belt somewhere.

"Where's all my…"

The guilty look on her face immediately gave her away and his momentary lapse of judgment induced by her "girl next door" outfit evaporated under the anger that licked its way through him. He took a deep breath, his hands clenching at his sides. She wouldn't have…would she? Who the hell did she think she was?

"Cherice…"

Her eyes widened at his use of her full name. She *should* have been worried. He hadn't been this pissed in a very long time.

"You had no right—"

"Just hang on. Before you go getting your chauvinistic

knickers in a twist, let me just explain."

He stopped at that. Okay, he could be an ass when he wanted to be, he'd give her that, but he didn't think he was chauvinistic. But hell, she could think whatever she wanted. She had no right to go throwing her money around whenever she felt like it. He wasn't some charity case.

"I know I'm not quite as well off as you are, Ms. Debusshere, but I'm perfectly capable of purchasing my own clothing."

She stiffened, the warmth fading from her eyes, her smile disappearing. "I never meant to imply anything differently. I just wanted to do something nice for you, that's all."

"How is buying my clothes nice? I'm not some charity project. I don't have any need or desire to be your good deed for the week."

Her eyes narrowed and she drew in a deep breath through her nose. He'd hit a nerve with that one. Good. How dare she treat him like some poor country bumpkin who couldn't even clothe himself without her help!

"You are such an insufferable ass!" she shouted at him, startling the cashiers and customers closest to them.

Oz blinked at her, momentarily surprised speechless. She shoved the bags containing his items into his arms.

"I was just trying to doing something nice—to say thank you for driving me. You paid for the car and you paid for lunch and the snacks and you didn't have to drive me in the first place. You could have just left me stranded there, but you didn't, so I just wanted to do something nice, so I thought maybe I could get your new interview clothes for you. That's all! I wasn't implying you couldn't afford to get your own clothes. And besides, it was easier to just toss your stuff in with mine. I didn't think it would be such a big deal."

Oz flinched. Even when apologizing she managed to show just how far apart they really were. She'd probably spent less on her entire haul than she did on a pair of socks at one of her usual stores. It didn't help that he *had* been a bit worried over the new outfit. He had the money to cover it, yes. But it really wasn't money he should be spending. The fact that it was about as momentous to her as buying a pack of gum dug at his pride.

However, there wasn't much he could do about it now unless he wanted to make her return the items so he could rebuy them. However, as good as that sounded, it would be a huge waste of everyone's time and a major slap in her face. Whether she understood what a slap in the face she'd just dealt him or not, at least he was pretty sure she hadn't done it intentionally. Besides, the customer service department was a total zoo.

Cher was eyeing him warily. He blew out a huge breath. He was still pissed, but she'd never understand why. And he didn't have the time or energy to try and explain it to her. He'd be better off explaining it to the soda machine they'd passed on the way in. At least then he was guaranteed to get something out of the conversation. Whatever. They needed to get moving.

He shifted the bags in his arms so he could carry them all in one hand, then reached out for the ones she held. She hesitated just a moment before handing them to him.

He nodded. "Thanks. I…appreciate the thought."

She looked like she wanted to argue but thought better of it. "You're welcome."

"Let's go before it gets too bad out there."

She nodded and led the way. But she didn't get much further than the doors.

The rain was coming down steadily in big, fat drops—it was like someone was standing on the roof aiming a fire hose at them. All the minor showers earlier in the day must have been a warm-up for the main event. The setting sun was trying to shine through the clouds and now the sky was a weird mustard color. Without saying a word, Cher reached into her bag and pulled out one of those cheap, disposable ponchos and held it out to him.

"Thought you might need one."

He snorted. "Thanks. Here." He handed the bags to her and took the poncho, slipping it over his head before taking them back.

Cher turned to him. "Can we drive in this?"

"We're going to have to, unless you want to spend the night here."

She shook her head but her brows were still puckered with concern.

"Come on," he said. "It'll let up in a few minutes. You know how fast the weather changes. We've been in and out of this the whole trip so far. Let's go."

Cher took off for the car, not worrying about the puddle this time, though it had grown considerably. Protected by her new foot gear, she stomped straight through it, looking so happy and carefree it took him a second to realize he was grinning like an idiot in the pouring rain, just staring at her.

He gave himself a nice mental slap and high-tailed it to the car. Cher jumped inside while he shoved the bags into the backseat, hurrying to the driver's seat as fast as he could. Truth be told, he'd rather not drive in the mess that was falling all around them. He didn't mind driving in the rain normally, but it was a total bitch when it was coming down so hard. But it should let up after a good hard downpour, and then it would be much more manageable.

He snapped on his seat belt and turned on the car. "We'll just take it slow. I'm sure it'll let up soon, and if it doesn't, we can find a nice bridge to park under."

"If you say so," she said, her eyes glued to the road in front of them.

"Try not to worry about it." His irritation with her dissipated a bit with the very real fear that shone from her eyes. "You want to listen to some music to take your mind off it?"

She shook her head. "Talking is better."

Well, that was debatable, but now probably wasn't the time to point that out.

She took a deep breath. "How about we get you ready for your interview? I can help you practice your responses. I'm pretty good at this kind of thing."

"You are?"

"Yes. I told you I do more than 'shop,' as you call it," she said. Her lips were smiling but one eyebrow was raised to let him know she hadn't forgotten that remark. "Interview prep is one of the things I do at work. It could help to run through some possible responses."

"I'm sure I'll be fine. I *have* done a few interviews before in my life."

"Yes, but some of these recruiters can be sharks. Especially in New York City. They are paid to weed out the weak links."

"So, you're assuming I'll be a weak link."

"I didn't say that."

"It was implied."

"It was not! Stop putting words in my mouth."

Oz sighed. "Okay, I'm sorry. Grill me."

She glared at him, obviously not sure if he was joking or not.

"I mean it. Go ahead and grill me. I probably could use an interview refresher. It's been a while since I've gone to one that requires a tie."

"All right. Who are you interviewing with?"

"Does that matter?"

He was reluctant to give her that kind of ammo. This was his dream job. And a long shot. He knew it. He just didn't want her to know it. He'd wanted to be a writer his whole life, had even gone to school hoping to eventually end up with a creative writing degree. Life responsibilities had derailed that for a few years. But now, a high-profile magazine was looking for a desk editor in his neck of the woods. It was a chance he couldn't pass up. To work for a big New York publication and still be able to stay at home…it was too good to be true. Definitely something he had to go for.

But the second he told Cherice, he knew he'd see that pitying look in her eyes. That *oh how cute, he thinks he can play in the big leagues* look that he'd been seeing on the faces of just about everyone he knew, once he'd gotten the interview. It was bad enough coming from his friends. He didn't want to deal with it from her.

She released a long suffering sigh. "I guess not, but I don't get what the big secret is. Anyway, first off, your handshake."

"Yes, walk in, look confident, firm handshake. I think that one is pretty well understood by most people."

"Yes and no."

He refrained from an eye roll. Barely. "Unless I'm planning on going in there and fist-bumping the interviewer, there aren't a whole lot of ways I can play this. It's a handshake. Either limp noodle or firm and confident."

"Not necessarily. You want a firm handshake, yes. But not too firm. Too loose, and like you said, you come off not confident. Too firm, you might come off as *too* confident, cocky, arrogant. Someone who won't take direction. Someone who has problems with authority. Too far the other way and you aren't outgoing enough, you won't take the lead. They want a go-getter but not a glory hog. And not a person who is desperately trying to pretend they are confident when they really aren't. It's all about balance with these companies."

Oz opened his mouth to argue but she actually made some good points. Go figure.

"What are you, the Interview Whisperer or something?"

Cher laughed and Oz found himself smiling along with her.

"Hardly. I've just been around my mother my whole life. She can size up an opposing counsel by their handshake alone. She passed on a few pointers."

"All right, Yoda, teach on."

Cher opened her mouth, blinked twice, and let the Star Wars reference go. *Hmm.* Bonus points for her.

"Okay, well, like I said, it's all about balance. Just like when they ask where you want to be in five years or what your future plans are. Yes, they are looking for someone who will be loyal and stick with the company long-term. And yes, they are looking to fill a certain position. But they don't necessarily want someone who wants to be in that same position five years from now. Nor do they want someone who is going to bail. They want someone with some ambition."

She stopped talking and pointed out the window. "We're crossing into Maryland. Aren't we going to stop and take a picture?"

Oz cocked an eyebrow at her. "I think we'll skip this one. I don't want to drown."

She grinned and shook her head. "Okay, so…where were we? Oh yeah, where do you want to be in the future? A safe answer would be something along the lines of how you are looking for a career, not just a job, and you hope that their company is one you can grow in, that kind of thing. That way, you aren't implying you will jump ship at the first opportunity, even if that ship is within the company, but you are still letting them know you are willing to work hard to get ahead."

Huh. "Never thought of it that way. I usually say that I hope to still be working for them, but never really articulated that I'm interested in being promoted."

Cher nodded. "That's not a bad answer, but showing them you have the drive to work hard enough to get ahead with them goes a long way, too."

Oz tried not to show his surprise at the brains she was displaying. Not that he'd thought she was just an empty-headed, spoiled shopaholic. Not totally. But the woman seemed to have some smarts. And that was sexy as hell.

"Pennsylvania coming up. Wow, that was fast."

Oz laughed. "We're just going through the corner of Maryland. It doesn't take long."

"Ah. No picture?"

"Not unless you found some scuba gear at the store you

didn't tell me about."

"Sorry," she said laughing. "So how much longer until we get to Montauk?"

"Six hours."

"I thought it was six hours last time I asked you. That was two states ago."

"No, it was about six-and-a-half hours last time you asked. It only takes about forty minutes from where we stopped in West Virginia to here."

"Oh. Are you going to stay in Montauk or…"

He shook his head. "I've got a hotel booked in New York. I'll drop you off and head back to the city."

She just nodded, leaving Oz to wonder how she felt about their trip coming to an end. Not that she really should feel anything in particular after only knowing him for a day. But still…it hadn't been quite as bad as he'd feared. Mostly.

"Hey…Thanks, Cher. For…all your help with all this."

Her cheeks flushed and she looked out the window. "No problem. It's no big deal."

"Yes, it is." The words he hadn't said to anyone regarding this job trembled on his lips. Saying them out loud made it more real, made it so much worse if he failed. Ah, the hell with it. "I really want this job, more than I've really wanted anything. I really appreciate your help. With the clothes and the interview prep. All of it. Thank you."

Cher beamed at him, that beautiful smile of hers lighting up her face. "You're welcome, Nathaniel."

An answering warmth spread through him, happiness like he hadn't felt in quite a while filling him.

Damn.

Chapter Eight

Cherice sat in a warm little bubble of happiness. Nathaniel had thanked her, and had seemed genuinely grateful for her help. The whole episode just helped solidify in her mind what she truly wanted to do with her life. What made her truly happy was her work with DressHer. Helping women find good jobs, teaching the seminars on interviewing and career building. It was something she loved to do. Something she'd love to continue doing.

She'd let Nathaniel think she was a personal shopper because she'd thought it'd be easier than the truth. He wasn't really wrong. She just hadn't trusted his reaction if he'd heard the whole thing. Maybe she should have. Maybe she would.

She'd love to open another location. The one she worked at offered a lot, but it wasn't set up to expand with more donations of clothes or other equipment, such as computers and printers, etc. If she were to open a location that stocked well-made, very affordable, stylish clothing, it would give their clients more options. She could offer business attire for women and men, and even prom or special-event dresses for teen girls. She could continue to teach the seminars but run the clothing store on her own. She would have everything her clients would need in one place at extremely affordable, even way-below market prices.

Calming relief spread through her. There was something freeing about knowing what she wanted out of life. It was weird to think it was thanks to Nathaniel. She was very well aware she'd been sticking her damn foot in her mouth the whole trip. Although it wasn't entirely her fault that he seemed determined to make everything about money. It didn't matter what she said, he twisted it to be some "rich person picking on a poor person" slam.

His face when he'd realized she'd purchased his clothes still made her cringe. She'd just wanted to thank him for helping her out. Looking back, it might not have been the best way to go about it. In her defense, she'd still been in a bit of a lust-crazed haze induced by his impromptu strip show.

It was just…wrong. He'd been laughing at her, though. Maybe it was just his way of getting her back for invading the dressing room. She had sort of asked for it. And if he wasn't totally off-limits, she'd ask for it again. That wasn't a sight she wanted to forget. Good gracious, it was criminal for anyone to look that good. Her palms were still sweating at just the memory of his bare chest, corded muscles tapering into the band of his slacks. She wanted to crawl inside his pants and find out what the rest of him looked like. And then lick every inch of him. Shame-filled guilt edged that thought out of her head before she could dwell on it too much.

Then again, Nathaniel's amazing body was a much more pleasant image to dwell on than the infuriated look on his face when he'd seen her standing there with those bags in her hand. Ox. Was it really so hard to graciously accept a gift nowadays? It would have served him right if she'd bought him some jammies and fuzzy slippers, too. Maybe a nice pair of tighty-whiteys.

She halted that line of thought in its tracks before it could get out of hand.

Still, he seemed happy with her now. And the sheer pleasure that spread through her at that thought was…disturbing. She tried to shove it aside. She liked that she'd made him happy. And she really didn't want to pick apart the reasons why, because she was pretty sure she wouldn't like it. And neither would his wife.

She was so going to hell.

The car fishtailed slightly and Nathaniel's hands gripped tighter on the steering wheel. Cherice's stomach somersaulted.

"What was that?"

Nathaniel kept his eyes glued to the road. "Just hydroplaned a little."

The rain was definitely coming down harder. It seemed just within the last minute they couldn't see more than a couple feet in front of them.

The car slowed down even more and Nathaniel flicked the hazards on.

"Nathaniel?"

"I'm trying to find a spot to stop. I can't see a thing. This will probably let up in a few minutes and we can get back on the road. If I can find a spot. I guess a sudden downpour sends everyone scurrying under a bridge, no matter what state you're in."

Cherice snorted. He was totally right. It was impossible to find an empty bridge or even a side of the road when the rain was really coming down. But if the under-the-bridge spaces were taken, that left them with few possibilities.

"All right. I'm just going to pull over to the side here for a minute."

Her stomach sank further and she sent up a quick prayer of thanks that Nathaniel had offered to drive her. The thought of being alone and trying to drive through this mess made her heart seize up.

He edged the car over as far as he could on the shoulder and shut off the engine.

They both sat staring out the windshield while the rain pummeled the car. The fat, heavy drops *pinging* off the car were unbelievably loud, sounding more like they were parked under a waterfall than on the side of the road.

"Well, this is fun," he said after a few moments. "Let's listen to the radio, see if we can find any weather reports." His mouth quirked up in a little half smile that made her heart skip a beat.

She was going to respond with some cute little quip when the car jolted, sliding in the mud.

Cherice screamed, panic shooting through her so quickly her head spun. Or maybe that was because the freaking car she was sitting in just slid off the road and it threw off her equilibrium. She threw her hands out to grip the sides of the car like that would somehow keep it from moving. "What was that?"

"Shit," Nathaniel said.

"What? Is the car sliding? It felt like it was sliding."

"I don't think it's going anywhere. I just pulled over a little too far. We're stuck in the mud."

"Are you kidding me?"

"Yeah, I figured now would be a great time for a joke like that." He turned the car on and tried gunning it, but the tires just squealed uselessly in the mud.

"Shit," Nathaniel said again, slamming the car into park. He grabbed his poncho out of the backseat. She started to reach for hers but Nathaniel held out a hand. "Stay."

He got out and slammed the door, hurrying to the passenger side so he could squat down to take a look.

"Stay," she scoffed, reaching for her own poncho and umbrella. "I'm not a dog, you big Ox. *Sit, Cherice. Stay, Cherice.* I don't think so."

Not that she particularly wanted to get out and stand in the rain, but she couldn't let him get away with that nonsense. She pushed the door open. It wasn't until she heard the startled *yelp* from Nathaniel that she remembered he was crouched down near the passenger-side tire. The door hit him with a sickening *thunk* followed by a muffled shout as he went sliding down the small embankment they'd parked next to.

"Shit," she whispered.

She popped open her umbrella and peered down the hill. Nathaniel lay on his back about ten feet away. Luckily the hill wasn't all that steep so he shouldn't have a problem climbing back up. Unless she'd knocked him unconscious.

"Nathaniel?" she called down.

Nothing.

"Nathaniel!"

He lifted his head and looked at her. "Oz."

"Oh, for crying out loud." Irritation and relief washed through her, along with a rush of adrenaline so strong her head spun.

Wait. She wasn't dizzy because she was relieved.

"Cher! Be careful!"

She tried to take a step back but she barely had time to shriek before the ground beneath her crumbled and down she went, rushing to the bottom of the hill along with a cascade of mud and water.

When she slid to a stop, she lay still for a second, taking inventory. First of all, rain boots, a poncho, and an umbrella offered no protection at all when caught in a mudslide. Secondly, the cute red sundress was now a soggy brown. *Ugh.* It was a really good thing she never went commando or she'd be in a world of muddy trouble. She'd never been so grateful for that thin silk barrier as she was at this moment.

"Are you okay?" Nathaniel asked, leaning over her, his hands searching her face.

It took her a second to drag some air back into her lungs past her furiously pounding heart, but the adrenaline was kicking in. She slapped at his hands.

"I'm fine. What the hell was that?"

"Mudslide. I guess parking in the mud wasn't such a great idea."

She didn't find it remotely funny. "You think?"

Deep down she knew it wasn't his fault but with the terror still flooding her system, and mud still flooding everywhere else, she wasn't in the mood to be fair.

"In my defense, I couldn't see where the asphalt ended in the downpour. Which," he said, holding out his hand, "seems to be letting up a bit."

She groaned and sat up. "Great. So instead of drowning we'll just get really wet."

Nathaniel got to his feet. "It could be worse."

"Oh really, how?"

He reached down and hauled her to her feet. "The car could be down here with us."

He climbed back up the hill, looked at the car, and then opened the back door, presumably so he could make a phone call without getting his phone wet. Guess it was a good thing the car was a rental, because they were both covered in mud and Cherice, at least, had no intention of standing in the rain waiting for whoever was going to come for them.

She started scrambling up the hill with her umbrella in her hand. Halfway up, she chucked the damn thing over her shoulder. Keeping dry was a bit of a moot point, anyway. When she was close enough to get a good peek at the tire, it had sunk even farther into the muck. Oh yeah. The car wasn't going anywhere anytime soon. Which meant neither were they.

Panic clawed at her. Her mother's fury when she wasn't there tonight and the very real possibility that they were in serious trouble had Cherice's body in a full tremor. Either that or the aching cold that was spreading through her. Usually it felt good when it finally rained during the summer. It broke the humidity, like a giant water balloon that had been sitting around sweating condensation finally exploded. So why was she cold? She shifted uncomfortably, her wet dress slapping against her bare legs.

Nathaniel was on the phone but turned to her with a frown when her teeth started chattering. It was a bit cool with the sun down, but not enough for that. Maybe her nerves had finally snapped. He finished his call and shoved his phone back in his pocket.

"The tow truck is on its way, but it might be a few minutes. He's on his way back to his shop with another car right now and then he'll be right out to get us. We need to hang something from the window to help him spot us."

He ducked into the car and rummaged through the bags, coming out with his new tie.

Cherice gasped and snatched it out of his hand. "You can't use that! It's for your interview."

"Well, unless you've got something better, we're going to have to use it. I guess we could use my new shirt, but I figured if I had to go into the interview missing an item of clothing, the tie would be the least noticeable. Then again, maybe it would help my chances if I walked in dressed in nothing but slacks and a tie…"

Cherice laughed which, judging by Nathaniel's smile, had been his goal.

But that didn't solve their sos flag problem.

"What about that other dress you bought?"

She shook her head. "Now that this one is ruined it's all I've got that's clean. Well, I've got a nightgown and the yoga pants, but they're black so…"

"Yeah, no help."

She sighed. "I've got something we can use. But you have to turn around."

"Why?"

"Because I'm wearing it and you are not going to watch me take it off, that's why."

"You watched me take my clothes off. Fair's fair."

"Nathaniel!"

"What?"

That eyebrow rose again and Cherice glared, waiting for him to do as she'd asked. He finally held up his hands and turned around, but his smile stayed in place.

She unsnapped her bra and pulled it, one strap at a time, out through the sleeves of her dress. It took a few minutes, and a few muttered curse words, since she was fighting against wet material, but finally, she got the damn bra off.

"Here," she said, holding it out.

Nathaniel turned back around and froze, his hand halfway extended toward it.

"Well? Will that work?"

He swallowed and took the white lace bra from her, his eyes flicking briefly to her liberated breasts.

He couldn't see anything, of course. She was wearing a nice red this time, not the white of her previous wet shirt incident, and covered by a poncho, albeit a see-through one. Still, the way he was staring at her was like she was standing stark naked in the middle of the road. And he liked what he saw.

He's married! She reminded herself for the thousandth time. Cherice sucked her lower lip between her teeth and folded her arms across her chest.

Nathaniel cleared his throat and nodded, his fist clenching around the material. Cherice trembled again, imagining all too easily his hand closing around her instead.

"This is perfect. Why don't you get back in while I get this rigged up?"

He ducked back in the car to snag a hanger from one of the bags and lowered the driver's side window a fraction of an inch. Cherice made no move to get inside the car.

Nathaniel straightened the hanger, threaded both straps of the bra through it, and jammed one end of the hanger through the crack between the window glass and frame. Within just a few minutes, Cherice's bra waved bravely in the wind.

Nathaniel turned back around and frowned when he saw her standing there.

"You really don't need to worry. We'll be fine. We've got enough gas to last until he gets here, so we can keep the heat going if you're cold."

"That's good." She still made no move to get in the car. "Are you sure our weight won't make the car sink farther? Or maybe make the car slide down the hill?"

"It'll be fine."

She shuddered. "It's like a tomb in there when it's not moving."

Nathaniel's eyebrow raised. "Are you claustrophobic?"

"A little."

He frowned, studying her. A song filtered out to them from the radio that was still playing. His face immediately cleared and he leaned in to turn up the sound. Blind Melon's "No Rain" blared from the speakers.

He held his hand out to her. "Dance with me."

"What? Are you crazy?"

He grabbed her hand and pulled her into his chest. "Maybe. But you don't want to sit in the car and I don't feel like just standing in the rain staring at each other. So let's dance."

He pushed her out, keeping hold of her hand so he could spin her back into him again.

"Nathaniel!" She laughed. "No."

He grinned and twirled her again. She looped her arm around his neck so she could hold on.

And they danced.

His arm snaked around her waist and drew her tight against him, rocking with her through one of the slower parts of the song. She let her other hand rest on his chest. She could feel him staring down at her. But staring at him while he held her in his arms would be too intimate. They could *not* go there.

Maybe a quick peek wouldn't hurt. She looked up. Met his gaze. His lips pulled into a lazy smile that made her heart skip over to high-five her lungs. Her breath hitched in her throat and she dropped her gaze.

So wrong, so wrong, so wrong.

He twirled, dipped, and swayed with her until she was breathless. Water cascaded down their faces and slipped into the neck of her poncho and she didn't even care. He spun her again and her laughter echoed through the air.

The rain let up a little and the moon was trying hard to break through the clouds. Once the rain completely stopped it was going to be miserably muggy. But for the moment, with the rain keeping the worst of the heat at bay, it was actually kind of pleasant dancing under the dark sky. In his arms.

The song ended, but Nathaniel didn't let her go. "Feel better?"

She nodded, not meeting his gaze. She wasn't sure if she was having a sudden attack of shyness, or just didn't trust herself to raise her mouth within a few inches of his. Because she was definitely feeling things she really shouldn't be feeling and she'd never been great at resisting temptation.

"Come on. Let's have a seat for a few minutes."

Cherice still wasn't certain she wanted to get in the car.

Nathaniel anticipated her argument. "Only the front wheel is stuck in the mud. The back wheels are on solid ground. We won't slide anywhere. I promise. We can sit in the back so we aren't putting any more weight on the front. Here, I'll even get in first."

He climbed in, shutting off the music and then leaning his back against the door frame and leaving one leg stretched out along the backseat. Then he looked back at her, his piercing gaze burning right into hers.

"Come here," he said, cocking a finger at her.

Cherice wasn't so sure what she feared more. Causing another mudslide or snuggling against the mouthwatering man who reclined in the backseat of the car, his legs spread, waiting for her.

"Cher, come here."

She took a deep breath and climbed into the backseat with him, pulling the door closed behind her. She leaned back against his chest, her body rigid. Not with cold. But with something much more confusing. And so, so wrong. *He's married, he's married, he's married*, she chanted in her head.

"There," he said, draping one arm across the back of the seat. "Now you can see the exit at all times. Does that help?"

She took a tremulous breath. It actually did help. As long as she kept her attention on the bit of sky outside and not on the very large, very warm man behind her, she should be fine.

"Yes. Thank you."

"My pleasure," he said, his voice shifting from its normal

tone into something much huskier and infinitely more sensual.

She trembled.

"Cold?"

"No," she whispered.

"Don't worry," he said, reaching under her poncho to rub a hand up and down her arm. "The tow truck will be here any minute. Let's talk. It'll keep your mind off all this."

"Okay. Sure. What do you want to talk about?"

"You," he murmured, somehow making that one word more erotic than every romance novel she'd ever read.

"Me? Why me?"

"Because, all I know about you is that you have a terrifying family and you want to be a life coach and they'd never approve. So, what do you plan to do about that?"

Okay, the inexplicable desire she'd been feeling started to fade. The man really knew how to kill a mood. That was good, she supposed. No moods allowed.

"What do you mean?"

"I mean, what are your plans for your life? You said your parents had wanted you to go to med school and they aren't too happy about your current job. So, if they aren't happy with what you are doing anyway, then why not just do what you want?"

She groaned. "You still don't get it. It's really not that easy."

"Sure it is. Just dip into that pile of money you've got stashed somewhere and go to school, or open your store or do whatever you have to do. It's not like they'll be *more* mad at you, right?"

"I don't know why you think I have some huge pile of money just sitting there waiting for me to play with. Yes, my parents are well off and help me out every now and then, I'll admit that. But for the most part, I've been on my own since I graduated from college. Even if I did have a stash of cash somewhere, I still wouldn't be able to just pick up and do whatever I wanted. I have a little more consideration for my family than that."

"So, you have no plans for your life except to wait and do whatever Mommy and Daddy tell you?"

Cherice pushed away from him. He drew his knee up so she was no longer resting against his leg, but he didn't move it off the seat. She turned to face him. "The problem isn't that I don't have plans for my life, it's that you don't approve of what they are."

His eyebrow raised. "I can't disapprove of something that doesn't exist. Sitting there waiting for someone else to dictate what you will do with your life isn't a plan, Cher. It's a cop-out. It's easier to let them tell you what to do then take a chance and maybe fail, again."

"Don't think you know so much about my life."

"I'm not wrong, am I?"

She sucked in a breath, fury burning through her. But some of that anger was aimed at herself. Because he was right. She'd never wanted to be a doctor, but not getting into med school had been a huge disappointment. It had completely derailed her whole life. Making a stand against her parents about the shop was going to be nearly impossible as it was, piggy backing on the MCAT failure. But if she failed again and had to come crawling back? No way in hell would she put herself through that.

But the alternative was just as terrifying. There were really only two ways she could be of use to her family. The first—become a hugely successful doctor/lawyer/professional of some sort and help build the family name and fortune. The second—make an advantageous marriage and increase her family's connections and prospects through her husband. She'd not made any progress on the first. The second made her physically ill. But she was pretty sure that was what her mother had in mind for her. And what better place to get that ball rolling than at her sister's wedding?

Her mother had made some vague comments about meeting some new people this week, and had name-dropped a certain doctor her father was thinking of setting up a practice with, on several occasions. Cherice had no doubt that her scheming mother had the perfect someone picked out already.

Someone who probably wasn't anything like the tall, blue-eyed walking orgasm who was reclining in the incapacitated car like he was the king and it was his castle. The married man whose eyes kept drifting to her free floating chest where her nipples strained toward him with every brush of his gaze. The man whose full lips were pulling into a sexy half grin that said he knew very well what she was thinking at the moment. And liked it.

"You never answered my question, Cher."

"Your question didn't deserve an answer. And my name is Cherice, Nathaniel."

"I prefer Oz, Cher. And my question does deserve an answer. You're just too chicken to answer it."

"Excuse me?"

"You. Are. Chicken. You are afraid to admit what you really want out of life. Afraid to go for it. Afraid to fail. So afraid that you'll just be miserable your whole damn life rather than take a chance."

"That's not true."

"Yeah. It is. Then again, maybe you don't even know what you really want. You're so used to being told what to do every step of the way that a genuine decision makes you completely freeze up."

"It does not."

"Oh really? You couldn't even drive to New York by yourself. You're more than old enough—"

"I'm only twenty-four."

"Fine. You were still too afraid to get yourself from Point A to Point B alone. It wasn't part of the plan. You've probably never stepped out of line your whole life, have you?"

Cherice glared at him but he kept right on going. Every word stoked her anger, made her burn hotter, made her want to scream at him, hit him, show him that he was wrong about her. Show him that she could take charge. That she could seize the moment, live her own life.

Her breath came faster, her head spinning with the mix of anger and adrenaline and sheer straight-up lust.

He was still talking. But that smile played around his lips. He knew exactly what he was doing.

"I've done plenty of stepping. Maybe I'm just not interested enough in you to show you the real me."

Oz snorted. "Nice try, but you know I'm right. In your whole life you've never stepped out of the perfect little box your parents stuffed you into. Never wanted to do anything"—he reached forward and traced her lips with his finger—"that might be remotely forbidden."

Cherice gasped at his touch and it took every ounce of willpower she had to keep from sucking that finger into her mouth. She couldn't seem to breathe past the pounding of her heart. Nathaniel's hand moved to cup her cheek.

"Step outside the box, Cher. You know you want to."

He moved closer, his lips a breath away. All she had to do was lean in…

Cherice gasped and jerked out of his arms, suddenly remembering the main reason this man was off limits.

Her hand flew before she'd even made the decision to slap him. Her palm cracked against his cheek, the sound echoing through the car.

"What do you think you're doing?" she screeched, as he grabbed his cheek with a gasp of his own.

"What do you mean, what am I doing? What was that for?"

"How could you? I bet you do this kind of thing all the time, don't you?"

"Try to make out with a crazy woman in the back of a rental car? Nope, sorry, first attempt for me."

"No, you jerk! Cheat on your wife! What do you do, look for strange women to offer rides to so you can seduce them?"

Nathaniel frowned, his eyes narrowing. "What the hell are you talking about?"

"You know exactly what I'm talking about so don't play dumb. I'm talking about you trying to use me to cheat on the poor woman who is stuck married to you."

He threw his head back and laughed.

Cherice's jaw dropped and she stared at him in horror. "What are you laughing at? This isn't funny!"

He just laughed harder. "You're right, it isn't funny. It's downright, fucking hilarious." He leaned back against the door, catching his breath. "Why do you think I'm married?"

"I saw your family, so don't even bother lying about it."

"You saw my family? At the airport?"

"Yes. The beautiful blond woman with curly hair and a little boy who was obviously your son —"

"My nephew."

"What?" Cherice froze.

"My nephew. Tyler. And my sister, Lena. They moved in with me a couple years ago because she didn't have anywhere else to go."

Well, if that wasn't the sweetest thing she'd ever heard. But wait. That meant… "So…you aren't married?" she asked, her voice nearly a whisper.

Because if he was single, that meant…a whole world of possibilities.

"Nope." That half smile was back. He reached over and brushed a lock of hair off her shoulder, letting his fingers linger, trail up her neck.

"You're single? Free to do…" She licked her lips and he sucked in a breath.

"Whatever I want."

"Oh."

"Come here."

She didn't wait for him to ask again.

She reached forward and grabbed his poncho, yanking him up to meet her. Her lips crushed against his and bless his heart, that aggravating, arrogant, know-it-all man, after a split-second hesitation, jumped right off the cliff with her. He wrapped his arms around her waist and hauled her onto his lap, shoving his fingers through her hair to keep her lips molded to his.

She'd meant only to kiss him quickly, just enough to show him she could be crazy and unpredictable. But the second her lips touched his, something short-wired in her brain. Nothing mattered but getting more of him. Her lips parted beneath his, inviting him in. He groaned and pressed her closer, his tongue dancing with hers until her head swam. His hand trailed up her side, the plastic of her poncho crinkling as his thumb just brushed the side of her breast.

She threw her head back, the touch setting her on fire. He kissed her exposed throat, nipping at the tender flesh beneath her ear. She arched against him, wanting more, wanting everything. And he seemed more than willing to accommodate.

Oh God, oh God, oh God, oh God. I'm kissing him. I'm not just kissing him, I am trying to suck his tonsils out and praying to God he'll do the same to me.

Nathaniel's hand gripped the back of Cherice's neck, angling her face better so his tongue could delve deep into her mouth, exploring every inch.

Oh, yeah. Just like that. Oh God.

What the hell am I doing? This is so wrong. Although. I'm single. He's single. He can do whatever he wants. So can I. But do I want this? I don't even know him. Oh God, I am making out with a guy I don't even know. Does that make me a slut? What if he thinks I'm a slut?

He leaned farther back against the door, pulling her on top of him. His hand roamed over her butt, squeezing the trembling flesh, pressing it tighter against the hot, hard length of him.

Holy shit, I don't even care. He can think whatever he wants as long as he does that again.

"Cher."

"*Hmm?*"

His lips trailed their way up her neck.

"You're thinking too hard."

His teeth grazed her chin. Pulled her earlobe into his mouth for a quick nip. She sucked in her breath, nearly sobbing at the sensation that shot straight to her groin.

"Am I?"

"Yes. You are. So tell yourself to shut up and just kiss me."

"I can do that."

"Good."

She straddled him, her hands digging into his hair, pulling him back to her. She kissed him like she wanted to devour him and rocked against him until he threw back his head and groaned. He gripped her hips and thrust against her. The hard ridge of his pants stretched tight over his rock-solid length rubbed against her soft, already wet center. She cried out, gripping his shoulders while she pressed against him. She tried to get her hands under his shirt, wanted to feel his skin against hers. But she couldn't seem to get past the damn poncho he was still wearing.

He was having the same problem. He grabbed her poncho in both hands and pulled, shredding it until it was nothing more than two scraps of plastic. Cherice tore at the poncho covering him, laughing in triumph when she finally succeeded in yanking it away. She grabbed his shirt and raised his arms so she could tug it off him.

Oh God, ohmyGodohmyGodohmyGod. It wasn't fair for someone to be so perfectly formed. She ran her hands down his chest, her body rocking against him of its own volition when his nipples hardened to little pebbles beneath her fingertips. She leaned down, the tip of her tongue flicking against one, and Oz jerked against her, his breath hissing in through his teeth.

"No fair," he groaned. "My turn."

He pushed her up just enough so he could get his hands on her. She arched her back, trying to thrust her breasts into his hands. If he didn't touch her soon she was going to cry.

"Easy, baby," he said, his hands skimming over her shoulders, gently pushing her sleeves down until he could slip a hand inside her neckline. One warm hand closed over her breast, lifting it from the still damp material. His lips trailed over her warm flesh. She gasped, grabbing the back of his head to hold him there.

His lips closed on a nipple and she—

"Sorry, folks," a man's voice said.

Chapter Nine

Cherice gasped and looked over her shoulder, screaming when she caught sight of a very embarrassed tow-truck driver standing near the car. She yanked her dress back up and scrambled off Oz's lap, trying to maneuver her way behind him.

He, of course, was laughing his fool ass off. He climbed out of the car to talk to the tow-truck man. At least he was gentleman enough to block the door with his body until she'd gotten herself situated. She really didn't want to get out of the car and face the tow truck guy, but she could hardly ride in the car while it was being towed.

Jerry, according to the name on his overalls, let her sit in the truck while he and Nathaniel checked out the car they'd just hauled from the mud.

Nathaniel bent down to look at the tire that had just been liberated from the muddy ooze. After a few minutes of poking, prodding, checking under the hood, and doing a bunch of other mechanically inclined things that she had no clue about, he gave the tire a good kick and walked toward the tow truck. That couldn't be good.

He opened the door and climbed in while the driver got the car ready to go.

"Not good?" Cherice asked.

Nathaniel sighed and ran his hand through his soaking wet hair. "No. Looks like the axle might be cracked. Jerry says there's a rental place right next to his shop but it's closed for the night. He's going to take us to a motel."

"But…my sister's wedding is *tomorrow*. And so is your interview. We need to get there tonight!"

"I know. But we're only four hours from Montauk. Jerry said he knows the guy who runs the rental place and he can get him to open up early for us. That's the best we can do. But if we leave at the crack of dawn, we'll still get there in plenty of time to get where we need to be."

Cherice tried to keep her freak-out under control. There wasn't anything they could do about it, so having a total and complete shit fit wasn't going to solve anything. Still, it might make her feel marginally better. Even as the panic of possibly being late (or missing!) her sister's wedding chewed at her, a more pressing concern presented itself.

"So, he's taking us to a motel?" she asked, trying to sound casual and indifferent.

Judging by the grin spreading on Nathaniel's obviously well-kissed lips, she hadn't fooled him at all. "Yeah, there's one just up the road here, not too far from the rental place. Jerry already called ahead to make sure they had a room open."

She licked her lips, unable to tear her gaze from his lips.

"That's awful helpful of him."

"*Hmm*," Nathaniel said, lifting his arm to drape around her. "It is, isn't it?"

She leaned in a bit closer, trying to get enough air into her lungs without panting. He leaned down, his lips so close. She just needed to reach up…

"Wait a second." She sat back. "*A* room?"

He grinned down at her. "Sorry. It's a small motel and we aren't the only ones having issues with the weather. They only had one left." He leaned in farther, and rubbed the bridge of his nose along her jaw line. His lips touched her ear, his warm breath blowing into it as he talked. "Looks like we're going to have to share."

Cherice tried to swallow past the sudden dryness in her throat. She should protest. Insist she get her own room. Make him sleep in the lobby or something. No, that was mean. But surely they had another room. They always have an extra one just in case, right? She barely knew this man. She could *not* spend the night with him. No matter how badly she wanted to.

But before she could argue, Jerry climbed in the truck, firmly wedging her in between him and Nathaniel. He was a kindly-looking older man with a bit of a pot belly and a dimple in one cheek that made him look like someone's sweet little old grandpa. He smiled at her, but his gaze wouldn't meet hers.

He cleared his throat. "All right, let's get you folks somewhere you can get cleaned up."

Cherice leaned closer to Nathaniel. He drew her in closer against him, but instead of making her feel better, all it did was remind her of what they'd been doing when Jerry had pulled up. And how they hadn't had a chance to finish what they'd started.

Probably a good thing. Good grief, she'd been about ready to have sex with a nearly complete stranger in the backseat of a car on the side of the highway. What the hell was wrong with her? Probably a whole lot because while she was embarrassed at having been caught, and knew somewhere deep down she should be ashamed of such "wanton behavior" as her mother would say, all she was really sorry about was that they'd been interrupted.

Nathaniel's thigh pressed against hers and she closed her eyes, her hand curling into a fist to keep from touching him. Poor Jerry had seen enough for one night. She doubted he'd appreciate her jumping Nathaniel in the front seat of his tow truck. She couldn't let that happen, anyway. That whole episode had been one crazy lapse of judgment. One she'd very thoroughly enjoyed. She couldn't even try to pretend she hadn't, when her body was still throbbing with need. But it would have been a huge mistake they both would have regretted. Better to leave well enough alone.

The neon sign of the motel loomed ahead and Cherice's breath caught in her throat. They were about to spend the night in the same room. She prayed to God it was a double room because if there was only one bed, she didn't stand a chance.

Jerry dropped them off. The place was about what she expected to find. Blinking neon sign proclaiming rates by the hour, night, or week. Leering attendant tossing Nathaniel a key, barely blinking at their bedraggled appearance. What kind of people was he used to that they didn't even register on his curiosity meter? At least the place seemed clean, if in desperate need of an update. There was even a counter with free coffee next to a candy dispenser.

Wait.

She peered a little closer. That was…holy hell. It was a condom dispenser. In the freaking lobby of the motel. Her cheeks burned. Both in mortification that she was spending the night in a place that felt the need to offer their clients such a…convenience…and at the fact that she was sorely tempted to take them up on the offer.

She glanced at Nathaniel who held up the key and smiled at her. "206. Let's go."

He held the door open for her and she marched past him, head held high, steadfastly refusing to look at the *thing* in the corner.

She followed Nathaniel outside, down a short hallway, and up a set of stairs. Their room was right over the office with the window facing the flashing neon sign. Not the best location, to be sure. Probably why it was the only room open. Nathaniel unlocked the door and went in first, flipping on the lights.

Cherice followed, glancing around, half afraid of what she'd find. Thankfully, it looked just like most hotel rooms. A bit shabbier than she was used to, maybe. But for all that, not too bad. Everything was threadbare but seemed clean and that was the important thing. Nathaniel dropped all the shopping bags they'd rescued from the car onto the bed. The one and only bed in the room. A king-sized monstrosity covered in some 1960s green floral nightmare.

Cherice swallowed, her eyes darting around the room. The only other furniture was a tiny table with two chairs, an old dresser holding an even older television set, and a

nightstand on each side of the bed. Nowhere else for someone to sleep. She walked into the bathroom. Tiny sink. Toilet.
Shower stall. Not even a tub she could maybe sleep in. They
were stuck together. For the night. In the same bed. God
help her.

"You can take the first shower," Nathaniel said from the
bed.

She leaned her head against the bathroom door, unable
to keep the image of him climbing into the shower with her,
body all hard and wet, pushing her against the wall, the hot
water cascading over them...

"Cherice?"

"Yes?" her voice cracked and she cleared it and tried
again. "Yes?"

He stepped into the bathroom and she jumped.

"You okay?"

"Yes. Fine."

He grinned. "Okaaay," he said, drawing the word out.
"Did you want the first shower?"

"Oh. No. I need to call my brother. You can go ahead."

"Okay. I'll save some hot water for you."

She nodded but made no move to leave. He whipped
his shirt off over his head and dropped it on the floor. She
knew she was supposed to do something but for the life of
her she couldn't remember. It was the first good, clear look
she'd gotten of him, standing in the full light, and damn, the
man did not disappoint.

"You're welcome to stay if you want," he said, his hands
drifting to the button of his jeans. He popped it open and
Cherice snapped out of it.

"Oh, no, that's...no, I'm leaving. Sorry."

She closed the door on Nathaniel's smug face and flopped face down on the bed. She was never going to survive the night. Maybe if she made a pillow barricade or something. She'd read once that the Victorians or Puritans or some old time people did that sort of thing when they stayed in inns so everyone could get a piece of the bed. Frankly, the way she was feeling, even a pillow barricade wouldn't stop her.

She snorted. How pathetic was it that she was so hard-up she was dying to molest some poor stranger in a seedy motel. Her mother would be so proud. Speaking of whom…

She pulled her phone out and dialed her brother's number. He picked up on the second ring.

"Hey, sis. You almost here?"

"*Umm.* Not exactly."

"What do you mean? If you left right after we talked, you should be just about here."

Cherice sighed and flipped back over, scooting up to lean against the headboard. "Yeah, well we ran into a bit of trouble."

"We? Who's we?"

"Well, there was this guy at the airport who got bumped from the flight, too, and since he was also going to New York he offered to give me a ride, so…"

Something clattered in the background, like he'd dropped something. Like a remote hitting the floor or…oh, it had probably been his Xbox controller hitting the coffee table. Wow. She really *had* shocked him.

"So you climbed in a car with a complete stranger on a thousand-mile drive? Are you out of your damn mind? He could be total psychopath!"

She sighed again and focused on keeping her voice calm

and soothing. Most brothers were protective. Twin brothers gold medaled in the event. "Nathaniel is perfectly nice. You know how I am about driving and he was going the same way. Besides, I didn't have a choice. He'd gotten the last car so it was either that or I wasn't going to make it there by tonight."

"You aren't going to make it, anyway, are you?" he said, his voice tight with anger.

Lovely. He was already riled. He was really going to love what was coming next.

"No, we're in a motel."

"Cherice Buchanan Dubusshere! Are you fucking crazy?"

Her calm tone apparently wasn't helping. She could almost hear the veins popping from his neck.

"Our car got stuck in a mudhole and broke...something or other. The rental place doesn't open until morning. What else were we supposed to do? Hang out in the car all night?"

"That would be better than staying in a hotel with some strange man."

Cherice didn't think it would be wise to mention that staying in a car with Nathaniel wasn't all that safe an idea either.

"Where exactly are you?" he asked.

"A tiny little town in Pennsylvania. I'm only about four hours away from home. I'll be there in the morning."

"I swear, if I didn't have to go to this damned rehearsal party, I'd drive out to get you. In fact, I have half a mind to do it, anyway."

"You would not. Mom would kill you if you ruined the party, especially to save my sorry butt," Cherice said, happy he seemed to be calming down a little, despite his threat to come get her.

"Oh, I'm sure if I told her that her youngest daughter was in some seedy motel in desperate need of rescue, she would hardly forbid me from going."

"Sure she would. She'd much rather I come to some horrible demise in West Hickbottom than ruin her precious weekend."

Elliot snorted. "Well, I'd just have to make sure I told her in front of her friends. Then she'd look bad if she wasn't concerned about you and she'd have to let me come get you."

"Ha! Maybe. But she'd never forgive you. It's bad enough I'm constantly on her shit list. You don't need to be there, too."

"Geez. Potty mouth. One little road trip and you're talking like a trucker."

She laughed. "Oh, shut up."

"So, who is this guy? You better be behaving yourself or I will tell Mom, no matter how mad it makes her."

She smiled and grabbed a pillow, hugging it to her chest. "You better not. Remember, I know who really stole her car senior year and put the huge dent in the door. And put the cigarette hole in the couch. And gave the dog a mohawk the day before the dog show."

Elliot mock gasped. "You wouldn't dare!"

"Ha! You rat on me, I rat on you."

"Fine. Play dirty."

"Only way to play."

"Very true." He must have flopped back on his sofa because the leather let out an audible creak over the phone. "But really, in all seriousness. You okay? Who is this guy?

I'm going to Google him."

"Oh my God, Elliot, relax. He's a good guy, very nice. He's been the perfect gentleman."

She could feel him watching her before she heard him. The shower water was still running, but Nathaniel stood leaning against the wall near the bathroom door, smiling at her. He wore nothing but a towel wrapped around his waist and that ridiculous pair of flip flops.

"Fine. If you say you're okay, I'll believe you. Seriously though, sis, if you need me to come get you, you just call me, okay? Mom will survive."

Her gaze was still locked with Nathaniel's. "I will. Thanks, Elliot." She licked her lips, wishing she was running her tongue down Nathaniel's chest instead.

"Yeah. You just get here as soon as you can."

"I will," she said, but she was no longer really paying attention to him. "I better get going. It's been a really long day. And I'm sure Mom is wondering where you disappeared to."

He snorted again. "Yeah, she'll be sending out the dogs soon. Take care, Cher-Bear."

She smiled. "I will, Smelliot. Love you."

"Love you, too."

She hung up the phone and dropped it back to the bed.

"So you think I'm a nice guy, huh?" Nathaniel said, smiling and folding his arms across his chest.

All that did was showcase his incredible arms. And chest. Which still glistened with water. Cherice concentrated on drawing air into her lungs.

"You have your moments," she said.

Nathaniel gave her a slow, sexy grin and stepped farther into the room. "I left the water running for you. It was kind of tricky to get the hot water going so I was afraid to shut it off."

"Okay. Thanks."

Nathaniel nodded and watched as she dug in the shopping bags for some toiletries, her pair of flip fops, and her nightgown. She hesitated before pulling it out. She always slept in something slinky and silky. It was comfortable and she liked the way it felt against her skin. It wasn't something she'd planned on wearing in front of Nathaniel. But it was either that or…nothing. And the nightgown was definitely preferable to nothing. Theoretically.

He saw the bit of silk in her hand and the slow spread of his smile burned through her like those lips were already brushing against her skin.

"I don't have anything else," she murmured.

He just smiled. "Enjoy your shower."

She hurried to the bathroom and closed the door, leaning against it when she was safely inside.

"Let me know if you want any help!" he called out.

Heaven help her. It was going to be a long, damn night.

Chapter Ten

Oz leaned back against the headboard, a smile still playing on his lips. She'd looked so happy talking to her brother. Carefree. Playful. With that sunshine smile lighting up the room. He was glad she had at least one person in that crazy family of hers that she could connect with. It made life a little less miserable to have someone like that.

He felt that way about his own sister. But with her it was a little more complicated. Since she and Tyler had moved in, there was also an underlying sense of obligation in their relationship. Not that he resented for one second the need to take care of them. The fact that he could help raise his nephew and make their lives easier made him very proud. But that sense of responsibility sometimes overtook their old easiness together. Bills and jobs and child care and house chores had replaced hanging out and just having fun.

He should do something about that. Maybe when he got home, they could all take a weekend and just go somewhere.

Relax. And if he got this job…he sighed and leaned his head back, closing his eyes.

The ability to fully support his family, with money to spare, doing something he would actually enjoy doing? He wanted this job so much he was afraid to acknowledge it.

The water in the bathroom shut off and reminded him of another thing he felt that way about. The memory of Cher straddling him, arching into his hands…well, if she came out of the bathroom at that moment and saw his towel standing at attention she'd know exactly how he felt about their little episode in the car.

And now they were going to share a bed. For the whole night. He'd never survive.

The bathroom door opened and Cher clicked the bathroom light off and took up residence near the wall where he'd been. The only light came from the two bedside lamps. Standing in their soft glow, her damp hair curling over her shoulders, the black silk nightgown poured over her, hugging her curves like it was painted on, she was the most beautiful thing he'd ever seen. And he could never have her. There was no scenario where the two of them made any sort of sense. No matter what happened between them on this trip.

He knew without even touching her that once would not be enough. She was already under his skin. If he made love to her, she'd be in his blood, his soul. And how could he walk away from that?

She seemed unsure of what to do.

He smiled and tossed the covers back from her side of the bed. "I'm not going to attack you, Cher. Come on, get in bed. It's been a long day."

She still hesitated.

"I promise I'll stay on my side. I'll even stay on top of the covers if you want to get underneath."

"No," she said, finally moving. She walked to her side and climbed in. "You don't have to stay on top. I don't want you to get cold."

"I'm okay," he assured her.

She reached over, shut the lamp off, and lay back with a sigh. He did the same. Neither of them moved, nor spoke for several minutes.

"Are you asleep?" she whispered.

"No."

"Me, either."

"I noticed."

"Are you tired?"

He was, but he was also acutely aware that he was lying practically naked in bed with a gorgeous woman who only two hours before had been literally ripping his clothes off. It was a bit hard to relax.

"Not really."

"Me either. I mean, I am. But…I can't seem to…"

"Relax?"

"Yeah."

"Me either."

"Oh."

"Oh."

Another moment of quiet passed before she spoke again.

"Nathaniel?"

"Oz."

She groaned and he chuckled quietly.

"What?"

"Why won't you tell me what job you're interviewing

for?"

He took a deep breath and slowly let it out. "Because if I tell you and I don't get it, it'll make it that much worse. And it's a total long-shot that I'll get it."

"Oh." She paused for a second before continuing. "But your sister knows, right?"

"Of course, she does. But I trust her."

"I see. And you don't trust me?"

Oz rolled to his side to face her and she looked up at him. The neon light burning through the drapes was just bright enough to light her face in a strange, pink glow.

"Cher, you've made it more than obvious just how un-suited for life in an office you think I am. I'm just a blue-collar man from a little hick town and New York City is no place for me and I don't even disagree with you. But it doesn't make it easier to hear. Especially when I'm headed into an interview for a job I want so bad I could spit. A job I am well aware I am probably not qualified for."

She rolled toward him, her face puckered in a frown. "I never said anything like that. And I didn't mean to imply any of those things either, Nathaniel. I really didn't. I think the company you are interviewing for would be lucky to have you. Truly. I'm...sorry if I ever implied otherwise."

"Thanks, Cher."

She smiled and his heart picked up its pace. Good God, but the woman was beautiful. "You aren't going to correct me on your name?"

She shrugged. "Somehow, I don't seem to mind it so much anymore, coming from you."

Her words were quiet, shy. And hit him like a fist to the gut. *What is she doing to me?*

"You know, you can call me Oz. I promise not to tell anyone. It'll be our little secret."

She giggled. An honest to God giggle that made him want to roll her beneath him and see what other adorable sounds she could make.

"Oz."

It was even better than he thought, hearing his name on her lips. "There you go. Didn't hurt now, did it?"

"Oh, hush."

He laughed.

"So. Are you going to tell me what job you're going for?"

He lay back against his pillows. Maybe it would be easier to say out loud if she couldn't see him.

"There's a magazine that is looking for a desk editor for their southern office. The position would allow for some article writing, too."

"Really?"

He braced himself for her laughter, her judgment. Something. But the only thing coming from her was silence.

"I know it's a long-shot," he said.

"Why?"

Well…at least she wasn't laughing in his face. That was better than he'd hoped for.

"I don't have much experience. I was the managing editor for my high-school paper and for college—for the two years I was there. And I've done a few things for our local paper—occasional articles. Just the local-interest stuff. What festivals are coming to town, what the town council decided to do about the pothole problem on Main Street, that sort of thing."

"Sounds fun."

"Well. I wouldn't go that far. But, it's writing, at least. Gets my foot in the door. And I can do it around my other jobs. I know it's not much compared to some of the other people who I'm sure are applying. But, when I heard about it, I had to try."

"What about your sister and nephew?"

"They're supportive. Lena knows I've wanted to write my whole life. This at least points me in the right direction. And it's something I enjoy and I'd be able to do it from home. I'd need to fly into New York every now and then for meetings, but the rest of the time I could live where I am. It's the perfect job."

"You've always wanted to be an editor?"

He rolled back on his side to look at her. She wasn't laughing. Didn't seem amused at all. Just genuinely interested.

"Yes. Well, I'd love to be a novelist, really. But that would be even harder to make a living at than writing for a newspaper or magazine. That, at least, I can get a steady paycheck for."

"Maybe. Depends on what you write, I guess. Erotica seems to sell well."

He laughed. "Oh sure. Oz the erotica writer. You know, it's not a bad idea. I've got lots of ideas."

"I'm sure you do," she said, her voice hitching a little.

The sound erased the remnants of his amusement. Maybe he should show her just how many ideas he had. He reached out and traced the line of her jaw.

"You know, I thought for sure you would laugh," he said, leaning closer.

She looked up at him, her breathing quickening. "I wouldn't laugh. I know what it feels like to want a life different from what you're living. To want something it feels like you can never have."

"*Hmm.*" He ran his hand through her hair, smoothing the strands, letting his hand roam over the bare skin of her shoulder. "Do you?"

"Yes," she said, though it came out as more of a gasp.

"It's been tough sometimes, with Lena and Tyler depending on me. I'm happy to take care of them. But I've had to give up a lot. It's why I've tried not to get my hopes up too high. I know what a long shot this is. But if I did get it… if I could do what I always wanted and take care of them at the same time…"

"You have to go for it," she said, rolling closer to him, arching a little when his hand skimmed down her back.

"Yeah."

"Oz," she said, her breath coming in short gasps.

He leaned over and nuzzled her neck. "Yeah?"

"Shut up and kiss me."

He didn't have to be told twice.

His lips descended and she rose up to meet him, her arm circling his neck, her body pressing against his. His tongue delved into her mouth, tangling with hers until she was trembling beneath him. Oz knew he was about to dive into the deep end of the pool without knowing how to swim, but he couldn't stop himself. And despite the warning alarms firing in his head, the last thing in the world he wanted to do was stop.

All the pent-up frustration from their interrupted interlude earlier that evening came rushing to a head and he groaned, rolling her on top of him. The fabric of her nightgown tore slightly when she tried to straddle him and she nearly growled in frustration. Oz laughed, low and deep. He knew how she felt. He'd already lost his towel and if he couldn't sheath himself inside of her, and soon, it was a damn safe bet he'd explode.

She reached down, grabbed a handful of material, and yanked, ripping it clear up her thigh. She slung her leg over him and settled back. He sucked in a breath, his hands gripping her thighs. She wasn't wearing anything under the nightgown. There was nothing between them. Her hot, wet flesh skimmed lightly over him and it took every ounce of willpower he had not to lift her and drive himself inside her right then and there.

Two problems with that scenario. One, he wanted this to last longer than five seconds. And two...oh God.

She seemed to realize their problem the same time he did.

"Do you have..." she asked.

"No. Do you?"

"No? What do you mean, you don't? Don't all guys carry one around in their wallets?"

"Well, obviously not all guys."

She shifted and the movement brought the tip of his dick so close to paradise he really could have sobbed. He gritted his teeth, sweat popping out on his forehead. She gasped, her thighs trembling, obviously having the same problem he was.

"Wait!" she said.

"What?"

"In the lobby. I saw a machine in the lobby."

"Are you serious? You want me to go down to the lobby and—ahhh!"

She rocked against him and leaned down to suck his earlobe into her mouth. "I want you inside me so badly I'm about ready to scream."

He knew the feeling. He rolled her over, shoving his hands in her hair so he could claim her mouth. Their tongues met, thrusting and twisting with each other the way their bodies longed to do. Her breasts pressed against his chest and he leaned away from her just enough so he could get a hand between them. He palmed one firm mound, rolling her nipple between his fingers until it beaded, taut and hard. She arched against his hand, panting, silently begging. His lips closed over her breast, sucking her nipple into his mouth.

She gasped his name, her hand grasping his hair to keep him captive where he was. "Oz! Please. Oh God!"

He groaned and ripped himself away from her, his dick throbbing so hard he wasn't sure he'd be able to walk down to the lobby. But stopping what was about to happen was not an option. Hell, he'd crawl to the damn lobby if he had to.

Oz gave her one last kiss and then lurched off the bed. He grabbed his jeans off the floor and yanked them on while she snatched her purse from the table and dug through it.

"Here," she said, slapping a handful of change into his hands. Coins went everywhere. He caught as many as he could and shoved them into his pocket, then reached out to drag her back to him.

They walked backwards, their lips fused together, their bodies glued to each other, until he bumped into the door. He fumbled for the handle, still not breaking their kiss. He finally got the door open and they broke apart, both dragging in ragged breaths.

"Hurry back," she said.

She stood there, panting, her silk gown torn high enough to give him a glimpse of what he was missing, her mouth swollen from his kiss. It was physically painful to leave her. But he was out of options. Because not claiming her was off the table.

"Don't finish without me," he said with a wink, then took off down the stairs as fast as he could.

Chapter Eleven

Cherice paced the room waiting for him to return. Her body burned for him. Somewhere deep down she knew this was a bad idea, but she didn't care. She'd toed the line, always. Her entire life had been mapped out to make her parents happy. Fine. She'd deal with them tomorrow. But this night—this one night was hers. To do whatever she wanted. And she wanted Oz with an intensity that scared the shit out of her. She just prayed that the damn machine in the lobby was fully stocked and that Oz came back loaded.

She didn't have to wait long. He hadn't been gone three minutes when the door opened and he came bursting back inside.

"Well?" she asked.

He grinned and held up a handful of condoms. Her eyes widened.

"Think you'll need that many, huh?"

"Well, a man likes to be prepared."

Her laughed choked off when he dropped the condoms on the bed and stripped his jeans. He was still hard and full, and he didn't take his eyes off her as he grabbed a foil packet and ripped it open.

She pulled the straps of her gown off her shoulders, letting it fall to a puddle at her feet. Oz froze.

"My God, Cher. You are unbelievably beautiful."

She smiled and came to him, taking the condom.

"Let me help with that."

She leaned forward and kissed his chest, trailing her lips down his rock hard abs with little licks and nips, until his sensitive head brushed against her cheek. She looked up at him with a little smile, and took him in her mouth.

He threw his head back, his breath hissing through his teeth. She drew as much of him in as she could, her cheeks hollowing as she sucked. Her teeth lightly grazed the velvety tip and he groaned.

"You keep that up and this will be over before we've even started."

She smiled, reveling in the rush of power she had over him at that moment. But she didn't want to end things quite yet. She was wet and aching for him. She rolled the condom on and slowly stood, dragging her hands up his thighs as she did.

His hand fisted in her hair and he crushed his mouth on hers, devouring her lips while he walked her backward. They broke apart just long enough to scramble onto the bed and then he covered her, his body pressing hers into the mattress, his leg nudging hers apart. His hand trailed over her thigh, alternately squeezing and lightly brushing her skin, working his way up to where she wanted him most.

When his finger slipped inside her she rubbed against him, crying out at the sensations wracking her body.

"So ready for me. So hot and wet. Is this where you want me?" he asked, his thumb circling her clit.

"Yes," she gasped, rocking against his hand.

Another finger slipped inside and she almost sobbed. "Oz. Please."

"Easy, baby. I know what you need."

She moaned in protest when he removed his fingers but she didn't have to wait long for what she really wanted. He reached down to guide himself into her and she sucked in a breath as he entered her, one exquisite inch at a time. She bucked beneath him, trying to draw more of him inside. He grabbed her hips and thrust, sheathing himself to the hilt.

He held himself still for just a moment, letting her body adjust to the full, hard length of him. She shifted beneath him, wanting to feel more of him, her body begging for him to fill her, thick and deep, over and over again. Their gazes met, held, burned. No one had ever looked at her like that. Ever. Like he could actually see her, the *real* her. And wanted her. As badly as she wanted him.

Her body tightened around him. A slow smile spread across his lips as he began to move. Cher's inner muscles were already beginning to quiver, the orgasm building with every retreat and thrust. She rose to meet him, their bodies finding a rhythm that built into something that had her clawing at the sheets.

"Oz!" she gasped.

He moved faster, pounding into her, his muscles straining above her. She wrapped her legs around his waist and his mouth closed over her breast. His teeth lightly grazed her nipple and she came apart, shouting his name as wave after wave of pleasure washed through her. Oz was just behind her, his rhythm faltering. Two more thrusts and he found his own release. He froze, both of them savoring the aftershocks rippling through them.

Then he slowly eased down, resting his forehead on hers, careful to keep his full weight off her as they both gasped for air.

He brushed her hair from her forehead and leaned down to kiss her, slow and lingering. One final, tender kiss, and then he rolled to the side. He kept an arm around her and drew her against him.

"You," he panted, "are absolutely amazing. Incredible."

She looked up at him with a smile. "I was just going to say the same thing to you."

He caressed her cheek, kissing the tip of her nose. "Beautiful."

"It's never been like that for me."

"*Hmm*?"

"I mean I've enjoyed myself. But that…that was…"

"I know," he murmured.

He hugged her closer and for a moment she just allowed herself to be cuddled. She couldn't remember the last time she'd felt so…content. Her body was languidly spent and pleasantly drowsy and still experiencing tiny little waves of pleasure every time she moved. That she should experience something so extraordinary in the arms of someone she barely knew…

Oh God. She'd had mind-blowing sex with a man she'd met that morning. Her mother would be mortified. Hell, *she* was mortified. Or…at least she should be. But it didn't feel like she'd just had sex with a stranger. How was that even possible? Maybe time moved slower on a road trip because she felt like she'd known Oz much, much longer. But no matter what it felt like, he *was* virtually a stranger to her. So what kind of person did it make her that she not only didn't regret what had happened, she very much wished she could do it again?

Oz kissed her forehead. "I'll be right back," he said, easing away from her and heading for the bathroom.

He didn't take his towel with him so she was treated to an excellent view of his backside as he strolled away. And moments later, she got another eyeful of the front side. Judging from the state of her new favorite appendage, Oz was wishing they could have a repeat performance, as well.

She sat up, clutching the sheet to her breasts. He grinned. Yeah, okay, maybe it was a little late to play the shy virgin, but it was one thing to flaunt your assets when the heat of the moment was burning hot and heavy and another entirely to just lie in bed and casually let it all hang loose. She wasn't sure she could pull that off. Not that Oz seemed to care, going by the sudden determination in his eyes and the swiftly growing appreciation he obviously felt for what he saw.

"You tired?" he asked.

She shook her head, not sure she could trust herself to speak.

"Good. Because I don't think I'm done with you just yet."

Desire shot straight to her core and she tried to suck in a breath. "Oz," she said, meaning to talk him out of whatever he was about to do.

Once had been all very well and good but...ah hell. He

stalked toward her, muscles rippling in the pink neon light. Whatever argument she'd been about to make completely vacated her mind, leaving nothing but a raging desire to leap from the bed and attack him.

Apparently, he had other plans. Just as he reached the bed, he grabbed hold of the sheet she held, lifted it, and dove underneath. She gasped, but before she could say anything else, his hands spread her legs wide, pinned them to the bed, and his tongue licked her opening from one end to the other, pausing to swirl around her newly aching clit.

The sensation overwhelmed her so much she jerked backward, knocking her head against the headboard.

"Ow!"

Oz popped up from under the sheet.

"You okay?"

Cherice rubbed her head, her laugh coming out choked and breathy. "Yes. You surprised me, is all."

Oz's grin reminded her of that cat from that Alice movie, amused and sinful, and up to no good. "Oh, you haven't even begun to be surprised, baby. I'm just getting started."

His head disappeared again and he set out to show her just how right he was.

Hours later, she lay awake gazing down at him while he slept. His face still held all his personality, even relaxed in sleep. She'd seen pictures of herself asleep. It wasn't pretty. Mouth open, drool hanging, hair going in a million different directions. But Oz was just…Oz. He even had a little smile on his face like he found everything amusing, even as he was dead to the world.

Cherice rolled over and grabbed her phone. Oz stirred a little. She froze until he stopped moving, then quickly clicked a picture. The night flash went off, but he didn't wake. She gazed at the picture, unable to keep the smile from her lips. She'd captured the perfect moment.

She put the phone away and snuggled back against him. He turned to her and wrapped himself about her. Cherice drifted off to sleep filled with a sense of peace and contentment she'd never felt before in her life. And would probably never feel again.

A sliver of sunlight shone through the threadbare curtains, right into Oz's eyes. He blinked and lifted his head, then smiled. Sometime during the night, he and Cher had draped themselves around each other. He was holding her to his chest, both arms wrapped about her. One of his legs was wedged firmly between hers and her arm encircled his waist. Her other arm…Oz wasn't exactly sure where it was. It must be squished between them. But she didn't seem to mind. Neither did he.

Of all the ways this trip could have turned out, waking up entwined with Miss Cherice Buchanan Debusshere in a dodgy motel in the middle of nowhere was not a scenario he would have dreamed up. Yet here they were.

He glanced at the bedside clock. 5:30 a.m. He'd set his phone alarm for 6:00. Jerry had said the rental guy was going to open at 6:30 for them and was just a few blocks down. They could get ready, walk down, and with any luck, be in Montauk by ten and he could be back in New York by noonish. He should just get up and get moving. But he didn't want to ruin the moment.

He'd seen the look in her eye when he'd come out of the bathroom the night before. It might not have been full-blown regret, but it had been something along those lines. The problem was, she wasn't wrong. It had been foolish, maybe, but he couldn't regret it. At the same time, he had no idea where they went from there. He'd never had a one-night stand with a woman in his life. And Cher felt *less* like a one-night stand than many women he'd been in actual relationships with.

But they made no sense together. They'd been at each other's throats the entire day. Even if that hadn't been the case, they barely knew one another. And what they did know was enough to prove they had no business being within a mile of each other, let alone in an actual relationship. But... he knew if she woke up right then and told him she wanted to stay with him forever, he'd carry her off into whatever sunset they could find and do his damned level best to give her a happily ever after.

He could tell the moment she woke. The moment all the absurd *what ifs* running through his head evaporated into smoke. Her body stiffened against his and she pulled away from him. She sat up, brushing her hair out of her face.

"Good morning," he said.

"Morning," she murmured back, refusing to meet his eyes. "What time is it?"

He held in a sigh. Back to reality. "A little before six. My alarm should be—"

The theme song from the first *Twilight* movie played out loud and clear. He grabbed his phone and silenced it as quickly as he could. He'd forgotten about that.

"I don't like waking up to those blaring alarm beeps.

That was the first song I came across." He was totally lying, but he wasn't going to admit he loved the piano song from a movie he shouldn't even know the name of, let alone use to wake up to every morning.

She wasn't laughing, though she did smile. "I like that song. It's pretty."

He froze. Something in common? Could you build a relationship on great sex and a love for all things sparkly and cheesy?

She climbed out of bed, tripping a bit over the trailing sheet she kept tucked firmly around her. "I, um, I'm going to go get ready."

She still wouldn't meet his eyes. Well, that answered the relationship question. Not that it needed answering.

Cher showered and dressed in record time, edging around him in the bathroom, mumbling responses whenever he asked her a question, not speaking, otherwise. The one time he touched her, standing behind her at the sink and running a light hand down her arm, she balked. Their eyes met for half a second in the mirror, her cheeks flamed scarlet, she gave him a shy smile (though what she had to be shy about after all the ways they'd had each other the night before was beyond him), and then she mumbled something and bolted.

The awkwardness was so thick in the room he finally stepped outside just so he could take a good deep breath. There were some decent-looking bagels and horrible coffee in the lobby. The desk man who had been on duty the night before was gone, so Oz had at least one thing to be thankful for. The condom machine still stood in the corner. Oz would never be able to look at one of those things again without reliving the night he'd just had. Hell, what was he thinking? He'd be reliving that night for the rest of his life. Nothing was ever going to top that.

He stacked a couple bagels on top of two cups of coffee and brought them back up to the room. Cher had her leg up on the bed while she fastened the strap of her new store-brand sandals. She'd changed into a soft-looking dress that wrapped around her waist to tie at the side. The light purple color reminded him of his new interview outfit. They'd match pretty well in their respective outfits. Too bad their clothes would be all that matched.

She looked up when he came in and quickly put her leg back down. He held up the coffee and food.

"Breakfast. Not great, but it'll have to do for now."

She took it from him with a shy smile. "Thank you, Nathaniel."

And he was back to Nathaniel. So much for progress.

He finished gathering their things and held the door open for her. A few short blocks and a stack of new paperwork later and they were finally back on the road. Cher hadn't said anything in nearly twenty minutes. He couldn't take it anymore.

"Okay, what's wrong?"

She looked at him, startled. "Nothing. Why."

"Why? Because you haven't said a word in almost half an hour. Something's got to be eating you. And I know it's not me because you'd be enjoying yourself a hell of a lot more."

She gasped, her eyes wide with shock and outrage. *There* was his girl. He tried to keep the self-satisfied look off his face.

"Do you have to be so crude?" she asked, glaring at him.

He smiled, trying to leer at her and watch the road at the same time. "I don't *have* to be. But it's a lot more fun."

Cher kept her face studiously turned toward her window. "I think I'd rather just sit in silence, thank you."

"Well, I wouldn't. We need to talk about what happened last night."

"No. We don't."

"Why not?" he snapped.

She groaned. "What's the point? We had a little fun. It's over and done with. We'll be in New York soon and we'll go our separate ways. So I really don't see why we need to talk about anything."

"First of all, we fucked our brains out for a good four hours. If you are having a hard time remembering that, I'd love to give you a recap."

Her gasp of shock quickly morphed into an eye roll, but at least she looked at him. "Oh, I'm sure you would."

"You're damn right I would. And so would you."

"Well, we'll just have to agree to disagree on that point."

Oz smiled. She could throw all the attitude she wanted at him. She was squirming in her seat just thinking about it, her face flushing several shades of red.

"There's nothing to disagree with, Cher. You loved every second of it."

Her stubborn little chin jutted out. "Maybe I was just faking it."

"If you did, you deserve an Oscar for that performance. Well, for all those performances. How many were there?"

"Just drop it, Nathaniel."

"*Hmm*, you called me Oz last night. In fact, you were

screaming *Oh God, Oz!* with your legs wrapped around my waist while I pounded into you."

"Nathaniel!" she gasped, either in shock or outrage. He wasn't sure which.

"What? I'm just trying to get my facts straight. According to you, nothing happened last night that we need to discuss. But see, I'm not in the habit of spending a mind-blowing night with an amazing woman just to have her pretend it never happened the next day. Maybe I was dreaming. For instance, did you or did you not climb on top of me and rub your hot, wet—"

"Nathaniel!" Her voice had an edge of desperation to it now.

He grinned. Sparking the memories was definitely doing the trick. She licked her lips and Oz shifted in his seat, his hands gripping wheel. Slight side effect he hadn't anticipated. His little game was backfiring on him. Because he was getting every bit as worked up as she was. No way in hell was he going to stop, though. They *would* talk about it or he'd go through the whole damn night in such detail she'd be soaking through those little satin panties of hers in no time.

"Just making sure I'm not the one with memory problems. I mean, did I imagine it, or was it you on your knees in front of me, sucking my dick so hard I almost came in that hot little mouth of yours."

"I hate you, you know that?"

He smiled grew wider. "No, you don't, baby. You might hate the fact that you lowered your precious standards so far as to actually spend the night with me, but you sure as hell don't hate what we did. Or we wouldn't have done it four times. Or was it five? Did the shower count?"

She crossed her arms, her hands gripping her elbows so tightly they were almost white. "Stop it, Nathaniel, I mean it. I have nothing more to say to you on this matter."

Oh, he had no intention of stopping. She was reacting exactly how he wanted her to. "Well, it's hard to know what to count. Should we go by orgasm or just actual penetration? I'm pretty sure there were two orgasms—at least—in the shower. I've still got your nail marks in my scalp from when I made you come using nothing but my tongue swirling around your tight little clit."

"I'm warning you…"

By this point, he wasn't sure if she was warning him to stop or *not* stop. Her voice was breathy, her fists were clenched in her lap, her legs pressed tightly together. Maybe she was trying to keep her orgasm from escaping. He was having the same problem. If he kept it up too much longer, pun totally intended, he'd need a new pair of jeans.

"I think my favorite was the last one, when you were curled up on your side and I took you from behind…"

"Shut up, Nathaniel!"

"I think you came so hard that time the people in the next room pounded on the wall."

She finally turned to him, her hands clenched into fists on her thighs. "You are such an ass! Bite me!"

"Yep, I distinctly remember you saying that last night, only you wanted me to bite you here." He reached over and flicked a finger against a nipple that was straining against the fabric of her dress.

Cher gasped, her hand flying to her breast. Only instead of blocking him, she moaned, her eyes closing as she massaged herself, her fingers kneading at the soft flesh, her fingers squeezing her nipple.

Holy shit. Oz's mouth went dry and the constriction of his jeans went from uncomfortable to cutting off circulation. Enough of this.

He jerked the car onto the exit they'd near passed and Cher shrieked, grabbing the *oh shit* bar and holding on for dear life.

"Nathaniel, what the hell are you doing?"

"Teaching you not to play with fire."

She glared at him. "Don't get mad at me if you can't take what you dish out."

"Oh please. Don't even pretend you aren't as turned on as I am."

"Dream on," she said, nearly panting.

"I don't need to. I know exactly what you look like when you are dying to come, Cher. And you are dying right now, baby. Aren't you?"

He slid his hand up her thigh. She didn't stop him. Far from it. Her breath hissed through her teeth, and she opened her legs wider for him. Her panties were soaking wet. He moved them aside so he could slip a finger inside her and she moaned and grabbed his hand, pushing him farther in.

He'd been teasing her but he hadn't realized just how well his little game had worked. She was already throbbing for him. The feel of her hot and wet, her muscles quivering around his fingers, had him desperate to pull over so he could plunge balls deep into her.

"Shit, Cher. Hang on."

They reached a picnic area and he turned down a little dirt lane that led further back into the wooded area.

"So, what?" she gasped, rocking against his hand as best

as she could. "You're just going to park the car so we can go at it right here in the woods like a couple of horny teenagers? Real classy."

Her indignation would have sounded more convincing if she hadn't been riding his hand for all she was worth, nearly sobbing at the need to have him inside her.

"I never said I was classy, baby." His thumb found her clit and he rubbed it in little circles.

Her legs clamped around his hand and she threw her head back.

"Ah! Oz!"

He slipped another finger inside and rubbed harder. They hit a pothole and she came, screaming his name. He could feel her muscles gripping him, clenching around his fingers and he groaned, needing to be inside her.

"What's the matter?" she asked when she caught her breath. "Is driving getting a little hard?"

She leaned over and unzipped his pants, slipping her hand inside so she could palm him, rubbing her hand the full length of him and back again.

He pulled the car off into a small shaded thicket where it should be relatively safe from sight in case there were any early picnickers out there.

He slammed the car into park and ripped his seat belt off.

"Get over here."

Chapter Twelve

Cherice didn't wait for him to ask her twice. Damn it, she knew she shouldn't be doing what she was about to do, but for the life of her she didn't care. In about two hours she would be walking into her parents' home, back into the place where everyone seemed to want to make her feel as crappy about herself as possible. She wanted one more moment before that happened. One more moment with the man who had made her feel good for the first time in a very long time. Not just good. Happy. Safe. Sexy. Powerful. She wanted more of it. More of him. And she was damn well going to take it.

She tore off her seat belt and climbed onto his lap, trying to balance her knees on the slivers of the seat his body wasn't occupying. He jammed his hands into her hair and dragged her face to his, molding their mouths together. She drank him in like he was the last breath of fresh air she'd ever breathe again.

His hands dropped to her thighs and pushed her skirt up. Oh, yes, this is what she wanted. What she needed. God, one brush of his hand and she burned for him. She hadn't made out in a car since high school and she planned on doing a whole lot more than that. His hand gripped her ass and hauled her against him. She could feel the hot length of him burning through the layers of clothes that separated them and she fumbled for the button of his pants.

He yanked aside her dress and his mouth closed over a nipple. He sucked at it through the lace that covered it and Cherice arched against him.

"Oz," she whimpered.

"Backseat," he said, trying to help her off his lap.

Her butt landed on the steering wheel and she shrieked when the horn blew. Oz laughed and gave her a push toward the back. She fell onto the seat and quickly looked around to make sure no one had heard the horn. She couldn't see anything but trees. Good. Because she wasn't sure she could stop even if they had an audience.

"Condoms?" she asked, as Oz clambered over the parking break into the back.

"Bag on the floor. Ow!" His head banged against the roof of the car and he looked like he had a knee wedged near the parking brake.

Apparently his six foot-something-frame wasn't built to cram itself into the backseat of a car, but he managed somehow. Cher had the condom out and ready to roll. She sat up to help just as he leaned down and their heads *cracked* together.

Cher lay back on the seat and giggled. "Oh my God."

He laughed and shook his head. Their amusement died

away as they stared at each other, chests heaving. She had one leg on the seat, knee bent, and she knew it gave him a clear view. And just to make it a little easier on him...she dragged her hand up her thigh, hiking her dress up as she went. His gaze followed her movements, his breath ragged.

He shoved his jeans down as far as he could and rolled the condom on. Cher crooked her finger.

"Come here."

He grinned and she reached up to grab a fistful of his shirt, pulling him down to her. Their lips met, their tongues tangling. They fumbled between them, each trying to get her panties off. They finally managed and Oz wasted no time driving himself into her.

Cher gasped and clutched at him, her nails digging into his back through his shirt. "Oh, God. Oz!"

He pulled out and thrust in again. And again. She held on to him, trying to find a rhythm with him when she could barely move. He braced a hand on the seat back, his other hand pinning her hip to the seat. He drove into her over and over. Cher nearly sobbed at the sensations he was igniting within her. She wanted to make it last as long as possible. But they needed to hurry. It was broad daylight and they were in the backseat of a car.

"Oz," she gasped.

"Come on, baby. Come for me."

He pounded into her again. And again. She arched her hips, drawing him as deep as she could, the orgasm building deep inside her. It rippled out in waves, her muscles clenching and throbbing. Oz moaned and slammed into her.

"Cher! Ah, baby!"

One more thrust and he half collapsed on her. She

wrapped one leg around his hip, keeping him captive while little ripples of pleasure still ran through her. He looked down at her and she smiled, reaching up to pull him down for a kiss.

His lips moved over hers, tender but insistent, taking as much as he was giving. Cher poured everything she felt for him into that kiss, everything she couldn't say. She thought maybe he was doing the same. Her head swam with the emotions rocking her.

How was she going to let this man go? This aggravating, arrogant, pain in the ass, wonderful man. How was she going to just walk away from him?

Cher's kiss turned desperate. Oz pulled away and smoothed her hair away from her face.

"Hey. You okay?"

She smiled at him. "Yes. More okay than I've been in a long time."

"Good." He grimaced a little and shifted off her. "I'd really love to lie here all day with you but my leg is cramping up."

Cher smiled, refusing to think of anything else but that moment. The rest of the world could come crashing in later. Oz used the last baby wipe to dispose of the used condom and then settled back against the seat, pulling her into his lap. He kissed her, his lips gently caressing her forehead, her cheeks, her jaw, her neck. He nuzzled against her, breathing her in. Her heart skipped at the painfully sweet tenderness of his actions.

She didn't say a word, just curled into him and he held her. For just a brief moment, she considered the possibility that Oz could be the one for her. That maybe they could make it work. She could go live with him, open her shop near him. Have dinner on the table every night when he got home and send him off to work every morning with a cup of coffee and a kiss. They could have babies and maybe get a cat. Or a dog. Or both. They could have it all. Have their dreams and each other.

It was a nice thought.

But that's all it was.

Part of her would love nothing more than to walk right up to her parents and announce that instead of reapplying for medical school or marrying whatever suitable man they'd dug up, she was going to open her own extension of DressHer and ride off into the sunset with Oz. The other part of her knew she'd never do it. They'd disown her on the spot. And as much as they drove her nuts and sometimes made her downright miserable, she loved them. They were her parents.

And the longer she sat there, curled on Oz's lap like they had some kind of future together, the harder it was going to be to leave him and go back to her real life.

Time to end the fantasy and get back to reality.

Oz hugged Cher closer to him, reveling in the fit of her body against his. She let him hold her for a moment, but then stiffened and pushed away. He looked down, eyebrows raised.

"I, um…just want to get some air. It's hot in here. And I should probably clean up a little before we get back on the road."

Oz smiled. "Yeah, we did generate a bit of heat, didn't we?"

She gave him a faint smile, leaned over to grab her bag, and opened the door. The fresh breeze was nice. It was warm of course, but still several degrees cooler than the car, and a morning breeze blew through the trees.

Cher walked off a short ways to a picnic table surrounded by trees and thick brush. Oz watched her, unable to keep the goofy grin from his face.

Maybe they weren't so different after all. Maybe it really could work between them. Especially if he got the desk editor job. It was a major step up. He'd be able to quit all his other jobs, just focus on what he actually wanted to do. Be able to take care of his sister and…anyone else who might come along.

He wouldn't be able to provide the kind of life she was used to, of course, but they'd make out pretty well for themselves. And she could go to school and get her master's in business and do what she'd always wanted. They might actually be able to make a pretty decent life.

He realized how sappy he was being, daydreaming about white-picket fences and all the fixin's with some woman he'd just met. But…well if they could overcome all the differences they had and connect the way they just had after only a day, he was sure they'd be able to make a relationship work. If that's what she wanted. And with the way she'd clung to him it was hard to imagine her being opposed to the idea.

Cher dug through her bag and pulled out a bottle of water and some other items. Looked like she was going to give herself a little sponge bath. *Hmmm*, maybe he could help with that.

He sauntered over, his heart rate kicking up a notch

when she propped her leg up on the table bench and her hand dipped under her skirt. He came up behind her and wrapped his arms around her waist. She stiffened and dropped her leg, moving away from him.

Um, okay.

"Just thought I'd come see if you needed any help," he said, trying for suggestive and flirty.

Cher wouldn't meet his eyes. "No. Thank you. I'm fine. Almost finished."

"Are you sure?" he asked, reaching out to rub a hand down her arm.

She flinched away from him. "No. I don't want help."

Oz frowned, her reaction stinging. What the hell? Five minutes ago she'd been curled up in his lap clinging to him like she never wanted to let go. Now he couldn't even touch her?

She put a packet of tissues and a bottle of hand sanitizer on the table, scrubbed at herself again, and wadded the used tissues up to throw away.

His gaze zeroed in on the hand sanitizer and his stomach bottomed out. He swallowed past the hurt and anger that were slowly filling him. Really? So, that's how it was? She wasn't just cleaning up; she was removing all traces of him from her body.

With fucking *sanitizer*.

What a colossal joke he must be to her. There he was, fantasizing about them being together and all she'd been af-ter was a quick screw with some blue-collar guy she thought she could use and toss away. He should have known better. Hell, he *had* known better. He'd just been so distracted by her little act that he'd forgotten. He'd be damn sure not to make that mistake again.

Cher grabbed more tissues but froze when she looked up and saw Oz's face. Yeah. Game was up. He knew what she was up to now. And if half of what he was feeling was showing on his face, then yeah, she should look concerned. She was lucky he didn't just drive off and leave her ass there. He wouldn't. No matter how badly she'd just used him, he'd never do that to her. No matter how tempting it was.

"Nathaniel?"

He snorted. "I guess I'm only Oz to you when you want a good fuck."

Her mouth dropped open but he continued before she could say anything. He had no desire to hear what she had to say.

"Hurry up with your decontamination process, will you? I've got somewhere to be."

"What? What are you talking about?"

"Drop the game, Cherice. I got the message, okay. You had your fun. Slumming with the guy from the wrong side of the tracks. I'm sure it'll make a great story at your next family get together."

"What? No, that's not what—" She looked down at the sanitizer in her hand and flushed.

"Save it. I'm not interested in whatever line of bullshit you feel like trying to feed me. Just hurry it up. I'd like to get out of here." He jerked his head at her. "Make sure you get all of my filth off your precious little body. It would be a fucking shame if Mommy Dearest found out what you'd been up to because you missed a spot."

She gasped and Oz almost—*almost*—apologized. He was a total bastard. But she deserved it. She'd used him.

Made him think she actually felt something for him. Hell, if she'd just wanted to fuck, he'd have been up for it. They could have had a good time without her totally messing with his head.

He shoved the hurt and anger down. He'd deal with the fact that he was totally lying to himself later. For now, he just wanted to get this trip over with, drop her off, and forget he ever met her. But, even as he thought it, he knew that would never happen. She was unforgettable. And he was screwed.

He leaned against the car, pulling in great lungfuls of air, trying to contain the roiling emotions in him. So he'd just gotten used for sex. Big deal. Most guys wouldn't complain. So what the hell was his problem? She was the epitome of high maintenance. He should thank his damn lucky stars she didn't want anything else from him and just move on with this life.

His phone vibrated in his pocket and he yanked it out. Lena. He wasn't in the mood to talk to anyone but he never ignored a call from her. She or Tyler might be in trouble. He took a deep breath and answered.

"Hey, sis. What's up?"

"Hey. You in New York yet?"

"Not yet. This trip has been one huge pain in the ass. I should be there in a couple of hours."

"Oh good. You'll have time to get cleaned up for your interview, at least. Remember, don't be nervous. You've so got this nailed. They're going to love you!"

He seriously doubted it, but she was sweet to say so.

"So," she continued, not noticing his silence. "Is that girl you're traveling with still a piece of work, or did you work a little Oz magic on her?"

He was saved from answering that one by a little voice shouting, "Uncle Oz! Uncle Oz!"

"Is that my little buddy?" Tyler was the one and only person who could make him smile no matter what was going on.

Lena groaned. "He wants to tell you something. Here Ty, but make it quick. Mommy needs to talk to Uncle Oz, too."

"Uncle Oz, I got to play at my friend Josh's house and he had this tree house and…"

Oz's mind wandered back to Cherice while his nephew extolled the virtues of Josh's new tree house, making the appropriate noises of appreciation at the right moments. She was taking an awful long damn time to clean up. She must want to be *very* thorough. He forced himself to pay attention to what Tyler was saying.

"That sounds great, buddy. We'll have to see if we can find a good treehouse tree when I get home, okay."

"Okay! Bye Uncle Oz! Love you!"

Oz smiled. "Love you too, buddy."

Hearing that little voice definitely helped get his priorities back in order. He had a family to take care of. Tyler and Lena came first. He needed to get Cherice out of his head so he could concentrate on his interview. Getting that job was the only thing that mattered.

"You okay, Oz? You sound…off."

Uh oh. His sister could always tell when something was up. "Yeah. I'm fine. Just tired. It's been a very long trip."

And wasn't over yet.

"If you say so."

"I say so."

She sighed. "All right, then. I'll let you go. Iris just got here. Tyler is going to go play with her nephew at her sister's house so we can have a little girl time."

Oz snorted. Lena and her best friend had been getting into trouble together since grade school. A little girl time with Iris was never a good thing.

"Behave yourselves. I'm not there to bail you out."

"Oh whatever. We haven't done anything that bad since before I had Tyler. We're just going to a movie or something."

"*Uh huh*. Be good."

"Yes, big brother. And you. Drive safe! And good luck on your interview!"

"Thanks. I'll need it."

"Oh stop it. They'll love you. How could they not? Everyone loves you."

Not everyone.

"Thanks, Lena. I better get going."

"Okay. Let me know how the interview goes!"

"I will. Love you."

"Love you, too. Bye!"

She clicked off and Oz put his phone back in his pocket, exhaustion eating at him. And he still had to deal with Cherice for the next hour or two. He silently vowed to drive as fast as he absolutely could without getting pulled over. This trip needed to be over with.

He got back in the car, started the engine, and rolled the windows down. The car smelled like sweat and sex. A few moments ago, that scent would have had him revved and ready for another round. Now he just wanted to erase it, and her, from his life.

And he'd keep telling himself that until he believed it.

Chapter Thirteen

Oz hung his head out the car window. "You clean enough yet? We need to go!"

Cherice cringed at the hurt and anger in his voice. Not much she could do about that, though, so it was probably better this way. She took a deep breath and slowly walked to the car. If she was going into enemy territory, she was going in looking confident, no matter how much her insides were quaking. But that didn't mean she was in a hurry to get there.

The look on Oz's face when he'd seen what she was doing would be burned in her mind for the rest of her life. It hadn't been what he'd thought. Well, in a way maybe. She *had* been trying to clean the smell of him off her. But not because it disgusted her. Not because she viewed their time together as slumming. Far from it. Their moments together were the best of her whole life. She'd remember them always. Hell, she was counting on those memories to get her through the miserable days ahead of her. Who was she kidding? The miserable *years* ahead of her.

And she just prayed to God she never ran into him someday in the future. She really didn't know much about him, including exactly where he lived. Just because they'd been flying out of the same airport didn't mean they lived in the same town. Anyone living in a two-hour radius used that airport. She just didn't think she could deal with seeing him after walking away now.

But despite that, she was still about to walk into her mother's house and she didn't want to smell like sex and latex. What girl would?

She'd hurt him though, and that was the last thing she'd wanted to do. But maybe it was for the best. It would make it easier to walk away from him if he was pissed off at her. Theoretically. Her throat ached with the need to cry, but she refused to let any tears fall. She didn't cry over anything, anyone, or any situation. It was one of her mottos in life. A shittier one, to be sure. But it had saved her a lot of hours of wallowing. Hell, if she had given in every time something miserable happened, she would've spent her entire life in the fetal position sobbing her heart out. Better to shove it down where it didn't hurt anymore. Far better to be numb than heartbroken.

That seemed to be easier said than done in Oz's case. Her feelings for him weren't so easy to discard. Maybe because she wasn't even sure what they were. She just knew how she felt when she was around him. And she liked it. Too much. It had been stupid to let her guard down.

Cherice barely had time to close the door and fasten her seat belt before Oz sped off down the lane. He didn't take as much care to miss the potholes as he had going in. After a few minutes of being tossed around she'd finally had enough.

"Okay, I get that you're pissed, but I'd really rather you just yell at me than try and shake me to death."

Oz didn't even bother looking at her. "My apologies if my driving skills aren't up to your stringent standards, Ms. Debusshere. I know all us blue-collar guys look alike to you, but as a janitor and mechanic, chauffeuring isn't part of my usual repertoire."

"Oh, give it a rest, Oz."

"Nathaniel. Only my friends call me Oz."

"Oh my God, are you serious?"

"Yes."

"What is your problem?"

"I don't have a problem."

"Look, I know it looked like I was—"

"Don't." His voice cracked and the lump in her throat was back with a vengeance.

He cleared his throat and glared at her before fixing his attention back on the road. "I told you. We've got nothing to talk about. Just drop it."

"Fine," she said quietly, guilt flooding through her so strongly her stomach roiled with it. "How soon until we get to New York?"

"Not soon enough."

They rode in angry silence for a full two hours before Cherice recognized where they were and started to give Oz directions to her parents' house. He turned when she told him, switched lanes when she said to, but didn't say another word to her. They were about fifteen minutes from her home when she couldn't take it anymore.

She was about to walk into full-blown shit fest. Her

sister's wedding was hours away. She'd missed the rehearsal dinner and was definitely throwing off her mother's carefully laid plans, which was enough to get her kicked out of the family as it was. Considering she'd avoided every major holiday for months, her mother had lots of criticism built up. She was pretty much guaranteed a miserable day.

Add to that the fact she was going to have to open that car door and walk away from Oz, forever, and the very thin thread holding her together snapped. In her entire life, he'd been the one person who had been able to make her feel like her own person, like a person worth something. Because of who *she* was, for her, herself. She might not ever find that again. Yes, it was ridiculous maybe to have fantasized even for a second that they might have something more, but they could have at least parted as friends. She would have found some comfort knowing he was out in the world somewhere, thinking kind thoughts about her.

But now, he wasn't even leaving that option open to them. He'd been giving her the silent treatment for nearly two hours. She would probably never see him again and *that* was the way he was leaving it between them. She couldn't. She wouldn't.

"You're a real ass, you know that?"

Oz jerked, his face flushing with anger. "I'm an ass? Are you kidding me? After what you pulled, I've been a fucking prince!"

"A prince? You call sitting there pouting like a pissy sixteen-year-old being a prince?"

His jaw dropped. "You think I'm pouting?"

"I know you are! We just spent the entire night and half the morning making love and now you're just going to drop me off without a word all because of some stupid misunderstanding—"

"First of all," he nearly shouted, his hands gripping the wheel so tightly she thought he might snap it off, "we didn't make love. We fucked. Good and hard. We had an itch and we scratched it. End of story. Making love implies there were some emotions involved and you made it very clear that was not the case."

"Why?" she nearly shouted, her anger, hurt and frustration beating against her temples in one continuous ache. "Because I cleaned myself off? Well excuse me for not wanting to walk into my mother's house reeking of sex and condoms! She already has it in for me and the last thing I want to do is give her even more ammo. It had nothing to do with you. I wasn't trying to get your *filth* off me, as you so eloquently put it. I just didn't feel like announcing to the most critical woman in the world that I'd just had sex!"

"Why not? You're twenty-four years old. Are you really that afraid that she might figure out that her little girl isn't a virgin anymore? Or is it more that you don't want her to find out you went slumming with some janitor from the sticks? I'm sure if I was some investment banker or real estate tycoon, she wouldn't care how many times you screamed my name. Hell, she'd probably throw you a parade. But for someone like me, naw, I just get to be your dirty little secret for the rest of your life. The one time you took a walk on the wild side."

She shook her head, her vision going blurry with unshed tears. "That is so not true."

"Yeah, it is. You know, maybe it's time you stopped being so afraid of your Mommy and start living your own life."

"Oh, what. Like you do? You haven't exactly been living your dream now, have you?"

He clenched his jaw, drawing in a deep breath through his nose. "No, I haven't. But it's been for a lot better reason than because my parents told me not to. And in case you've forgotten, I *am* going for what I really want. Too bad you are too goddamned chicken to do the same thing."

"I am not—"

"What's the gate code?"

She looked around and realized they'd arrived. Panic clawed at her, and she wasn't sure if it was because she was about to face her family or because she was about to walk away from Oz. No matter what insults they'd been flinging at each other, the thought of never seeing him again filled her with a desperation she couldn't begin to understand or deal with.

She gave him the code and he eased the car through, pulling to a stop in the roundabout near the front door. He looked out the window at the sprawling three story Tudor style house surrounded by perfectly landscaped grounds, complete with a huge stone fountain in the courtyard.

He just shook his head. "Don't forget your stuff. And don't take all day about it either. It's going to take me a couple hours to get back into the city. I can't be late."

Cherice stared at him, her hands clenching in her lap. "That's it? That's how you want to leave it?"

"What I want has never been an option." He leaned over and pushed her door open.

She inhaled a deep breath through her nose, trying to keep the tears at bay. She wasn't even sure why she was so upset. He was right. What she wanted had never been an option for her, either. Ever. Why should this time be any different?

She reached into the backseat and gathered up her belongings. "Fine. Have a nice life, Nathaniel."

He snorted. "Yeah. Been nice knowing you."

She climbed out and slammed the door. He was halfway down her driveway before she had a chance to release her pent up breath.

The front door opened and Cherice closed her eyes, bracing herself for the next few days.

"Cherice! You made it!"

She breathed a sigh of relief and turned to find her brother jogging down the stairs. He was almost as tall as Nath... The Ass Who Would No Longer Be Named. He'd started sprouting muscles around eighteen, and now, at twenty-four, he had the broad shoulders and lean, well-muscled body of a swimmer. His light brown hair was spiked and gelled into an artfully messy hairdo that had probably taken him the better part of the morning to achieve. He scooped her up when he reached her and gave her a jostling bear hug.

She laughed, completely unable to resist his enthusiasm. As usual. Elliot could make a shark victim smile while the shark was still chewing on his leg. Cherice was still half convinced she and Elliot had been adopted. She couldn't figure out, for the life of her, how her parents had produced kids like them.

"Put me down, you goof," she said, swatting at him with her bags.

He let go of her and took her bags. "Where'd the guy that drove you go? I wanted to meet him."

Cherice gritted her teeth. "He had to get back to the city.

Doesn't matter. Not like I'll be seeing him again."

Elliot looked at her, eyebrows raised. He'd always seen through her. Twin intuition, maybe. And he was definitely more curious than she wanted to deal with. Before he could ask her any excruciatingly uncomfortable questions, she grabbed his arm and steered him up the stairs.

"So, how's it going in there?"

He groaned. "You had the right idea not showing up until the last second. The rehearsal dinner was a nightmare. Nothing was up to Mom's standards. She hasn't stopped talking about how if she had been in charge she would have fired the caterers and hired a different decorator and chosen a different location. And now she's on our cases. Dad's gone through three tuxes and even Grandmother got reamed this morning."

Cherice didn't hide her surprise at that news. Her grandmother was generally the one person her mother never crossed. "What heinous crime did she commit to deserve that?"

"I don't know. They were using a lot of really big words I didn't understand. Like cerulean, and ultramarine, and I swear they said something about a peacock but I have no clue what they meant. I thought Dad had nixed all the birds. All I know is that Grandmother had the wrong whatever it was and now she's trying to rectify the situation."

Cherice nodded. "And that is exactly why I am lucky to be a bridesmaid and just went with the dress Mom picked out."

"Yes, and it was the only smart decision you've made concerning this wedding," her mother said, stepping out of her office off the foyer.

Elliot gave her hand a squeeze. "I'll go put your bags in your room."

"Thanks," she murmured. Time to face the music. Or the firing squad, as it might be.

"Hello, Mother," she said, walking toward her mom.

Jacqueline Grace Buchanan Debusshere looked her daughter up and down. "You look tired."

From a normal mom, that might have been concern. From Cherice's mom, it was a scathing criticism. One did not ever appear in public as anything less than radiantly put together.

"It was a long trip," Cherice mumbled. Long, emotionally, and physically, draining. Not that her mom would ever find out those sordid little details.

Her mother sniffed. "Saying I told you so would be redundant and I don't have time for that today. We need to leave for the chapel in…" She checked the gold Rolex strapped to her wrist. "Exactly six hours and twenty-three minutes. I suggest you rest a bit before then. It wouldn't do to show up at your sister's wedding looking anything less than your best. You've neglected your bridesmaid's duties enough as it is. The least you can do is look the part. Besides, you never know who you may run into."

A bolt of dread sank right into the pit of Cherice's stomach. She got out of there and escaped to her room. Her gorgeous peacock-blue dress hung from a hook near her closet. If it was one thing her mom had in spades, it was good taste. The dress was incredible, and she'd look fantastic in it. And that had probably been the point.

She'd be willing to bet more than the entire bill for her sister's wedding that her mother's idea of Mr. Right would be sprung on her at some point during the night. And she would be expected to be polite and gracious and warmly welcoming. Bile rose to the back of her throat just thinking of it.

She curled up on her bed, exhaustion lapping at her. She was drained. Done. Maybe if she just closed her eyes for a minute…

She must have dozed off, though it hadn't felt like her mind had stopped for a second. The sun was lower in the sky and while she was still tired, her eyes no longer had the gritty feel behind them.

The nap hadn't helped the turmoil in her head. *He* hadn't left her thoughts for a second.

Even before she'd met…*him*…the whole set-up situation with whoever her mother thought would be perfect for her had been unpleasant. But now? Since she was never going to see you-know-who again, it was safe to admit, at least to herself, that no one was ever going to measure up to him. And it wasn't his handsome face or the rock-hard muscles she wanted to chew on like candy. Or even the way his eyes twinkled when he was trying to rile her up. Or the tender way he'd touched her after they'd made love.

He'd believed in her. He had barely known her, but he'd seen something in her that she hadn't seen in herself. He made her feel strong, powerful, like she could actually take control of her own life and do a good job running it. Even more than that, he'd encouraged her to go after what she really wanted. Hell. That was an understatement. He'd downright dared her to do it.

She flopped on her bed and glanced at the clock on her nightstand. 4:15. He'd be at his interview. Going after what he wanted. Trying to make his dream come true. Doing what he'd said she was too chicken to do.

He was right. She *was* chicken. An ultra-petrified, twice-frozen nugget of pure and unadulterated fear. No preservatives added.

She sat up and went to her desk, opening the laptop that sat there. The bookmark she'd looked at more times than she could count was right at the top of the list. The website for the University of North Carolina at Chapel Hill. She clicked on it and it opened to an application for the master's program for the school of business.

Her information was there. All filled out. Just like it had been for the last year.

The cursor hovered over the Submit button.

She had the money to go. She had the grades to get in. She just needed the courage to do it.

Cherice took out her phone. Opened the picture gallery. Clicked on the picture of him…Oz… she'd taken when he'd lain asleep next to her. His face relaxed, heartbreakingly handsome, charming, and goofy even in sleep. She smiled, a strange mixture of hope, excitement, and abject terror filling her.

She looked at the picture one more time. Then, with Oz's voice ringing in her head, she clicked the button that would finally put her on the road *she* wanted to be on.

Chapter Fourteen

Oz sat in the lobby, waiting for the secretary to call him in. He looked around the room, knowing he didn't have a chance in hell of getting hired. The two guys to his right chatted about their current freelance gigs, casually dropping names of awards they'd won, clutching file folders or thumb drives full of the proof of their labors. Two more guys and four young ladies sat spread around the office. All waiting for their interview. All looking comfortable in their suits—surrounded by all the steel and glass and chaos going on down on the street thirty stories below them.

He'd known it would be stiff competition, but this was ridiculous. He'd also been fully aware of how different New York City would be from his small town. But he hadn't realized how much he'd miss the quiet streets and laid-back atmosphere of the South. His grandmother had been right. The Yankees were all a bunch of loons. And she'd been one, before marrying his southern-bred grandpa, so she'd know.

Oz smoothed down his new purple tie, making sure it was straight and neat. As if that would help.

The door to the office opened and a young woman in a smart black pantsuit came out, a confident smile on her face. She smiled, shook the hand of the interviewer, and left with her head held high. The fluorescent lights shone on her chestnut hair in its tight, stick straight pony tail, and his heart slammed against his ribs. It wasn't Cher, of course. But for just a second…

Oz sighed and leaned forward, resting his elbows on his knees. He didn't know what it was about that woman. He'd known her a day. Yet there was just something about her that had grabbed hold and wouldn't let go.

The secretary glanced down at her clipboard.

"Nathaniel Ozeranski?"

He stood up. "Oserkowski."

The woman frowned at him. "This way."

She led him into the office and closed the door behind him. An older gentleman sat at the desk. He didn't even look at Oz when he came in; just flipped open a folder that looked like it contained Oz's resume.

"Mr. Oser…um…"

"Oserkowski," Oz said, taking a seat.

He didn't even get to break out the handshake that Cher had gone to such depths to teach him. Or use anything she'd taught him. It was clear from the moment he'd taken a seat he wasn't what they were looking for. The man barely asked him about his admittedly inadequate experience. Never made eye contact. Barely glanced at him. Asked him a few rote questions and ended with a, "Thank you for coming in today, Mr. Um…Nathaniel. You'll be hearing from us."

And then he bypassed a smaller stack with only three files and placed Oz's file on a larger stack. The reject stack.

Oz stood, swallowed his disappointment, and left before he could do something really ridiculous like try and get the obviously uninterested man to at least pretend he had a shot. He walked out of the office and went straight to the men's room, ripping off his tie as he went. He leaned against the counter, looking at himself in the mirror.

He'd known his chances were slim. He hadn't been completely delusional. But he had hoped his work would stand out for itself. Yeah, so okay, there wasn't much of it. But what was there was good. He thought he'd at least get a fair shake. But it was incredibly clear he was not what they were looking for.

Despite the crushing disappointment flooding through him, the thought most prevalent in his mind wasn't the jackass he'd just left in the office. It was the fiery brunette who irritated the crap out of him and insisted on calling him Nathaniel. He wrapped his tie into a ball with a small smile. How in the world had that woman gotten him to wear purple? He was crazy for still thinking about her. She'd made it abundantly clear there was no future for them. Although… her explanation of what he'd seen had made sense. Honestly, if he'd been walking into his mom's house he'd have done the same thing. But there were other issues. He'd have to be insanely masochistic to want to go back for more.

He shoved the tie in his pocket. Apparently, he was a total and complete idiot. She was right. He didn't want to leave things the way they had. He was a raving lunatic. Liked being kicked when he was down. Right in the nuts. Because not only had he just lost his dream job, he was about to go back and lose his non-dream girl. Again. But he couldn't leave without at least seeing her one more time. He needed something good to hold on to from this nightmare trip. And for better or worse, he hoped she was it. If not, well, at least he wouldn't spend the rest of his life wondering.

First, he'd stop off at his hotel and ditch the duds. He felt like a trained monkey in the suit that apparently hadn't fooled anyone, anyway. Then he'd go see if he could get rejected for the third time that day.

Cherice's mother blinked at her, drawing in slow, even breaths, outwardly calm. Cherice wasn't fooled. The only thing saving her was the courtyard full of people they barely knew but were desperate to impress. It was also possible that she'd finally done something so unforgivable her mother was stunned into speechlessness. Not probable. But possible.

Her father glowered at her and then waved a hand at her mother. "You deal with this, Jacqueline. I need to speak with Judge Carlisle."

Her mom didn't even watch him go. All her furious attention was focused on her youngest daughter. Cherice was surprised she didn't melt on the spot.

"Listen up," her mother said, stepping closer and vaguely smiling at some acquaintance passing by. "I do not have time for any of this nonsense right now. You are not going back to school like you are some high-school brat who has a shot at doing something with her life. You had your chance. You blew it. I left you to your own devices, as you wished, and you chose to be a personal lapdog who spends her days helping other people get jobs but can't seem to get one of her own."

Cherice wanted to defend herself. But her mom wasn't wrong. She had blown it. Repeatedly. Maybe she had used up her second chances.

"Time and again I've tried to give you the freedom you wanted, and you've made one poor choice after another. Look at your siblings. Look at what they've done with their lives. Lilah is a successful surgeon who just married an even more successful doctor and Elliot has made the Debusshere Charity for Children one of the most successful in the city. And what can you say? You've changed your mind *again* and want to start all over? Go back to school for some degree you'll never be able to use, certainly not to amount to anything. Waste more time and money? No. This conversation is over."

Arguments bubbled up in her mind. Reasons why going back to school was a good idea. Reasons why opening her own shop could be beneficial. For her and her community. Why it wouldn't be a waste to do something she really loved—that could benefit so many.

She couldn't say any of it, however. It wouldn't matter. Her mother had made up her mind. And maybe she'd be better off doing what her mom wanted. Her siblings had, after all, and look at how well their lives were turning out. They weren't screw-ups.

A cold calm spread through her, grim acceptance of her fate. She was so tired of fighting. What was the point?

"Yes, Mother."

"Good. Now," she said, gripping Cherice's arm and turning her to face a group near her father. "You see that handsome young man by your father?"

She gave yet another acquaintance a fake smile and raised her champagne glass in response to their congratulations. Cherice's stomach knotted and she took a sip from her own glass to try to ease her nerves. The battle lines had been drawn. And she wasn't going to win this one. Her throat grew tight and she took another drink.

Her mother either didn't notice her distress or didn't care. "That is Dr. Jonathan Fitzgerald. He and his father have been discussing opening a new practice with your father. I'm sure I don't need to tell you how advantageous that would be for us. The Fitzgeralds are the most influential doctors in the city."

Cherice knew what was coming. She downed the rest of her champagne and handed the glass to a passing waiter while grabbing a full one.

"Don't get too drunk, dear. By all means, do what you need to in order to loosen up a bit. But don't overdo it. Jonathan likes his women bubbly and cheerful, but he certainly doesn't want a lush."

A tiny spark of defiance reared its head.

"You can't seriously expect me to marry some stranger just to make sure a merger goes through."

Her mother patted her arm, her attention on the people wandering about the tented wonderland that had been erected for the reception. "Don't be so dramatic, dear. Of course you won't be getting married right away. We have to make the man like you first. So do try to be likable, will you? Oh, and first thing in the morning, you call that school and withdraw your application. You'll be much too busy for that nonsense. Jonathan's family has invited us to their villa in

Majorca. We leave next week."

Cherice stared open-mouthed at her mother. "I haven't even met him yet. We might hate each other."

"Not if you play your cards right. And I'm sure you will, won't you?"

Cherice didn't say anything. A touch of what might have been pity or compassion or maybe even a tiny bit of motherly concern lit her mother's eyes for the briefest moment. "I know it might not seem fair at the moment—"

"Fair?" Cherice scoffed.

The soft emotion faded from her mother's face, leaving the perfect social matron back in its place. "But, I really do have your best interests at heart. Jonathan is young, handsome, and extremely successful. He's quite the catch. What more could a woman want?"

An image of Oz laughing after he'd made her squirm or that wink when he'd just done something he knew she wouldn't like invaded her mind. What more could a woman want? How about a man who actually cared what she thought? What she hoped and dreamed? Who not only cared but had done what he could to make it all come true for her?

Oz had been the only person in her life, except for maybe Elliot, who had even pretended to care about what she wanted. Yes, they got on each other's nerves and seemed to come from two different planets. But at least he seemed to genuinely care about her. And it had lasted for a whole twenty-four hours. The best day of her life, if she was honest with herself. Most certainly the best night.

She had never experienced passion like that with anyone. Ever. And she couldn't imagine ever doing so again.

The memory of that night, and this morning, were burned into her mind forever. She almost laughed. If she went along with her parents' plans, the hours she'd spent with Oz were quite possibly the only moments of true intimacy and passion she might ever experience. And they'd been in a dingy motel with a condom machine in the lobby *and* the backseat of a car. How utterly sad was that?

Her mother took her silence for agreement and left her alone to make her rounds of the guests. Cherice backed away, moving to the periphery. The tent opened up so guests could wander about the botanical grounds. Clumps of plants had been set up along intervals to keep people from wandering too far. She found one where she could still keep an eye on the majority of the party while staying relatively secluded. She didn't want to be bothered but felt better being able to keep an eye out for either of her parents.

It was a warm night but she shivered. Elliot stopped by her little corner a few times and tried cheering her up, but even he couldn't coax a smile out of her. The despair seeping through her was too great this time. A rustling behind her caught her attention and she turned, not sure she wanted to see who was there. She hadn't seen her parents or Jonathan for a few minutes. The last thing she wanted was to be cornered by them.

"Cher?"

She spun around. Her breath caught in her throat. What was he doing there?

"Oz," she breathed.

They stared at each other for a moment, neither one moving or speaking. Then he opened his arms and for once in her life she didn't hesitate.

Oz wrapped his arms around her, completely bewildered. Cher burrowed against his chest and he held on even tighter. What the hell was going on? He'd expected to get thrown off the property the second she saw him. *This*...whatever this was...hadn't even entered his realm of possibilities.

"Sorry," she said, pulling away from him. "I didn't mean to..."

"No worries. You can run into my arms anytime," he said, giving her a little wink.

Her lips twitched into some vague resemblance of a smile but it couldn't erase the misery from her face. He'd never seen her so beaten, not even at the airport when she thought she'd had no options. Even then she'd been full of spit and hellfire. But now. He'd never seen anyone who had well and truly given up...until that moment.

"Hey," he said, tucking a strand of hair behind her ear. "What's going on?"

She crossed her arms, whether to hug herself, or to keep from hugging him again, he wasn't sure.

"Nothing."

"Ah, come on. Anyone could see that's not true. And I'm not just anyone."

Her startled gaze met his and he got a little more of a smile.

"It's nothing. Really. Just"—she waved at the reception going on beneath the tent—"my family."

"Ah. That bad, huh?"

She turned her head so he couldn't see her face. "You could say that."

"Is it your mom? Was she really that pissed that you were late?"

"No. She…it's just…"

Her voice cracked and Oz reached for her. "Hey. It's okay. What's going on?"

He tried to pull her into his arms again, but she resisted and he didn't push it. The way she was staring up at him, her eyes searching his face, almost panicked, made him want to round up every last member of her family and beat some sense into them.

"Cher," he started. But that was as far as he got.

She launched herself at him, grabbing fistfuls of his T-shirt to drag him down to her. Her lips met his with an eagerness that left him reeling. He'd never been so confused in his life. But with her lips moving feverishly over his, her tongue thrusting into his mouth, he wasn't about to question it. What the lady wanted, the lady got. Good motto to live by.

She flung her arms around his neck and he wrapped his arms around her and lifted her until her toes barely skimmed the ground. They came up for air only to get a better angle before molding themselves together again. He poured every ounce of tumultuous emotion he'd been feeling over the past twenty-four hours into that kiss. She had to be doing the same. He could feel the desperation, the passion, and most of all, the promise behind the kiss. A little hope sparked in his heart.

His hand cupped the back of her neck. The other skimmed down her back toward her ass to press her closer until he realized that they were probably visible to at least a few of the partygoers. He tried backing them up, but ran into a bush. They needed to get somewhere a little more private so he could kiss the lady good and proper and really explore where this might be going.

"Cher," he said, pulling his lips away just long enough to get her name out. "Baby, we need to move…"

Her hand threaded into his hair and she pulled him back to her lips. He didn't fight her.

"Cherice?"

The woman's voice calling her name had the effect of dumping a bucket of ice on Cher's head. She gasped and pushed away from him, hurriedly straightening her clothes and patting at her hair.

"Your lips," she hissed.

He lifted a hand and wiped, assuming there must have been traces of her lipstick on them. There wasn't time to do anything else. A moment later, an elegant woman in a deep blue dress rounded the corner with an older gentleman in tow, and a younger, much less snooty version of the man close behind them.

Oz straightened, holding himself up to his full stature. These had to be Cher's parents. And her twin brother, maybe. Judging by the general pleasantness and happy twinkle in the guy's eyes, Oz guessed he must take after some distant relative because he certainly didn't act like the rest of the family.

"There you are. We've been looking all over for you. People have started to notice your absence."

Her mother's glare switched to Oz and he was hard pressed not to squirm. Ten seconds in her presence and he understood Cher a whole lot better. It was a wonder she didn't have *more* issues growing up with this woman as a mother.

"Who is this?" she asked.

Cher jumped. "I'm sorry. Mother, this is Nathaniel Oserkowski. He was kind enough to share his rental car with me. Nathaniel, these are my parents, Jacqueline and Claude Debusshere. And my brother, Elliot."

Her voice softened a bit when she introduced her brother, but as for the rest, she could have been introducing some random cab driver to the queen of England. She didn't betray by so much as a glance in his direction that he meant anything more to her than that. She stood rigid, her gaze not meeting anyone's.

Elliot stepped forward to shake his hand with a smile. "Hey man, thanks for driving her. She's terrible at driving. I swear, she'd get lost—"

"Elliot," her mother said. "Will you please find your grandmother and tell her it's almost time for the toast? She's probably wandered off again."

Elliot gave his mother a confused look and Oz was willing to bet his Christmas tips that the woman already knew good and well where Grandma was. Elliot didn't argue, though. He gave Oz and Cher a sympathetic smile and left.

Mr. Debusshere looked Oz up and down, gave him a curt nod, and then walked away, pulling his phone from his pocket to answer a call. Her mother looked back and forth between the two of them, her face growing harder if that were possible, at the sight of Cher's mussed hair and faded lipstick. He resisted the urge to wipe his mouth again and stared back at the woman. No wonder Cher was so terrified of her. He wanted to pick Cher up and carry her away from these awful people, protect her from them.

But they were her family. And she'd shown no sign that she wanted him to do that. Hell, she was acting like she didn't even know him at all.

Mrs. Debusshere's delicate nose wrinkled like she'd just come across something foul. "Thank you for your service, Mr. Oserkowski. If my daughter hasn't already done so, I will see to it you are adequately compensated."

Cher cringed but said nothing.

Oz frowned. "I do not require any compensation, Mrs. Debusshere."

"Very well, then. I believe you can find your own way out. Cherice, it is time for the toast. We've kept our guests waiting long enough."

She took Cher's arm and led her away. Oz watched, helplessness warring with outrage in his chest. He'd been dismissed, no mistaking that. And he would be happy to leave. But the thought of abandoning Cher to these people made him want to upchuck all over the bitch queen's azaleas.

But they weren't some criminals holding her hostage. They were her family. If she had shown any sign of wanting to go with him, he'd rip that woman's claws from Cher's arm and hide her away where they could never get to her again.

Just before they turned the corner, Cher looked back at him. That fiery light that had shone from her eyes was gone. Snuffed out completely. And he finally understood. It was over. That kiss hadn't been a promise of all the things to come. It had been a goodbye. Not just to him, but to everything she truly wanted out of life. She'd given up. Game over.

His Cher was gone.

Chapter Fifteen

Oz sat on the hood of his car, his phone in his hand. He needed to call his sister and tell her how the interview had gone. She'd been texting him non-stop for the last two hours and had called twice. He also needed to get his ass in the car and get on the road. He'd been planning on staying the night nearby and leaving in the morning, but now he just wanted to put as much distance between himself and New York as possible.

He climbed into the car and dialed his sister.

"Nathaniel Leopold Oserkowski, I'm going to kick your butt when you get home! Tyler and I have been on pins and needles all afternoon waiting to hear, haven't we, buddy?"

"Go Uncle Ozzy!"

Lena laughed. "See? So, how did it go? They loved you right? Of course, they did, who wouldn't? Tell me!"

Oz waited until his sister ran down. There was no getting any word in edgewise when she was hyped up about something. Which, under normal circumstances, was kind of great. Nobody could cheer you on the way Lena could. But when things didn't go so well, it sometimes made the disappointment that much harder to deal with.

"Well…" he said.

"Oh, no. Really?"

"I wasn't what they were looking for, but they wish me the best of luck."

"Those idiots don't know what they just let slip through their fingers."

Oz sighed. "I'm sorry, Len. I knew it was a long shot, but I thought I had at least some kind of chance."

"You've got nothing to be sorry for, Oz. Not a thing. Don't you worry about it. Something else will turn up. And if it doesn't, we're doing just fine. I just wanted this for you. I hate to see you working so hard all the time."

"Yeah. Well. It's for a good cause," he said with a slight smile.

"You're a good man, Oz. Don't you ever forget that."

"Yeah, yeah."

"When are you coming home? You going to hang around out there for a while? Do some sight-seeing? Maybe see some more of that woman you rode with that you refuse to tell me anything about?"

He knew she was just teasing him but her words slammed into his gut like a sledgehammer. "No," he ground out. "I just want to get out of here. I'll see you guys tomorrow."

"Okay," she said, sounding faintly surprised. "Well, travel safe and make sure you check in. Don't make me start calling the hospitals."

"Yes, ma'am."

"Love you, Oz."

"Me too! Me too! Love you Uncle Oz!" Tyler shouted from the background.

Oz laughed. "Love you guys, too. See you tomorrow."

He hung up and leaned his head back against the head-rest. There would be other jobs. Sure. There probably would be. Maybe even better jobs with more money and more along the lines of what he wanted to do. But with his lack of experience, it was pretty safe to assume those opportunities would all end the same way. He was just a blue-collar guy from a middle-of-nowhere town and that is all that people saw when they looked at him. No matter what kind of fancy clothes he was wearing.

He looked down at the passenger seat, frowning when he spotted something on the floorboard. He reached down and snorted. The damn hand sanitizer. He chucked it into the backseat, but couldn't get rid of Cher's image so easily. He could still smell the light jasmine scent of her on his shirt.

He understood the whole sanitizing episode now. Good God, did he. If that woman had been his mother he would've dipped himself in battery acid to avoid a confrontation with her. He'd overreacted and he'd been an ass to not let Cher explain. And, with his last thoughts still on repeat in his mind, he realized he'd also been the worst kind of hypocrite.

He'd spent nearly their entire trip razzing her about not going after what she wanted, being too afraid of what her family would think. Letting that fear stop her. And what had he been doing his whole life? What had he just made up his mind to keep on doing because of one disappointment? How could he expect to deserve an incredible woman like Cher if he couldn't even believe in himself first? And how could he just give up and walk away from her without a fight?

She made him feel like he could take on anything. In fact, not once had she ever actually said he wasn't worthy of her, or of a better job, or of anything. In fact, *she* was the one who had encouraged *him* while they had prepared for his interview. She was the one who had cheered him on. And here he was, ready to give up, because of one stumble. Sure, he and Lena were making ends meet just fine in the meantime. But he was tired of just making ends meet. He was tired of working three jobs so they could just manage to get by.

That wasn't living. That was surviving. It never really bothered him before, but now? Now he wanted to *live*.

And he didn't just mean his career.

He wanted Cher.

The incomparable, irritating, irresistible Cherice Buchanan Debusshere. More than anything he'd ever wanted. Including that damn job. And he was pretty sure she wanted him, too. She'd said that they'd made love, and she'd been right. It hadn't been just some cheap one-night stand, no matter what he'd said in the heat of his anger. He wanted *her*. The whole package. He wanted to see if they could build something together. Wanted to at least give them a chance to explore whatever they'd been feeling. *He wanted her*.

The disgust on her parents' face ate at him. He was not good enough for their daughter. Not by a long shot. But he got out of the car anyway. Though he had about as much chance of getting his girl as a one-legged chicken in a horse race, he wasn't leaving without at least making an attempt.

Cher sat at the head table, watching her father deliver a toast to the happy new couple. Of course they were happy. They were the perfect couple, with the perfect jobs, who'd married the perfect people their perfect families approved of, who were about to start their perfect lives together. Living in the perfect house in the perfect neighborhood raising their perfect 2.4 kids. It was the life Cher had been raised to want. The life she could have if she just followed her parents' perfect plan, married the perfect doctor they had picked out and lived perfectly ever after.

But she didn't want that. Had never wanted it. And now that she'd seen what she could be missing, the thought of having anything less destroyed what little of the real her was left. She didn't want perfect. She wanted messy, and annoying, and inappropriate, and so unbelievably passionate it made her tremble just thinking about it. She wanted happiness. But she'd left happiness, or at least the promise of it, standing alone in the bushes, her kiss on his lips and her parents' unspoken insults ringing in his ears.

A tear slipped down her cheek and she ducked her face to hide it. Elliot reached over beneath the table and took her hand, squeezing it gently until she looked at him. His face was creased with worry. He'd never seen her cry. No one had. She didn't cry. Ever. She'd always seen it as synonymous with exposing her jugular. It was a weakness that she'd refused to indulge in. But now, she couldn't help it. Another tear followed the first. And another.

Elliot handed her a napkin so she could dab at her face. He slung an arm around her shoulders and dabbed at his own pretend tears, eliciting some chuckles from those seated nearby. She gave his hand a squeeze in thanks and held her breath to stop the floodgates from opening.

She managed, barely. She kept the tears at bay, but not the miserable thoughts that wouldn't stop running through her mind as her father droned on about what was truly important in life.

He had it so wrong. What difference did it make that they were getting a good start in life because they had their careers well in hand? All the thinly veiled jokes about the country club and promotions and how they could go on their honeymoon later because they were too busy right now were just...rubbish. Depressing.

Her sister and her new husband laughed politely, but Cher wondered how they truly felt about how they were starting their lives together. She knew they loved each other. Oh, they'd never be so crass as to actually indulge in any inappropriate public displays of affection. Like playing tonsil hockey in the bushes while their guests danced on by. But she could tell by the way they looked at each other that there was genuine love between them.

Lucky them. They'd managed to fall in love with someone from the right gene pool. But there they sat, at a huge wedding that neither of them had any hand in planning, postponing a honeymoon so they could get right back to work building their empires, instead of taking some time to focus on each other, on their new lives together.

That was so sad. And the thought that the same fate awaited her? Only without the benefit of actually loving the man she'd be shackled to for life? The lump grew in her throat again and she took a deep breath, trying to pull herself together. This was what her family had reduced her to. A blubbering mess with a broken heart and shattered spirit.

No, not her family. Herself. She'd allowed it. Everything they'd done. She'd sat back and just let it happen.

The lump in her throat faded away and she sat up a little straighter. She was responsible for her own happiness, not them. They'd never been concerned about what would make her happy. Despite their dictatorship over her life, she knew her parents did care about her, were trying to ensure her future the best way they knew how. But it wasn't what she wanted. Not by a long shot. And they were never going to understand or support that.

If she wanted something, no one else was going to give it to her. She was going to have to go after it herself. Go after *him*. And if she hurried, she might just catch him before he crossed the state line and she never saw him again.

There was a sea of tables between her and the exit. There was no way to just sneak out. But she couldn't wait. Oz was getting further away with every second. Cher squeezed her brother's hand again.

She leaned over to whisper in his ear. "I love you, Smelliot." She kissed his cheek.

He looked at her, his eyes questioning. She just smiled. "I have to go."

She didn't know what he saw in her face, but whatever it was had him beaming with approval.

"Yeah you do. I'll deal with the fallout. Get out of here."

She didn't hesitate any longer. She pushed away from the table and got to her feet. Her father stopped mid-toast to stare at her open mouthed.

"Cherice," her mother hissed. "Sit down!"

"I'm sorry, Mother. But I have somewhere I need to be."

She ignored the gasps and muted giggles and wound her

way through the tables, one single thought burning in her mind.

Oz.

Oz's heart pounded in his chest but he didn't stop to re-consider. He knew what he wanted and no one was going to stop him. He marched into the reception tent and stopped short. Gasps and whispers erupted all around him. Cher's father stood at the head table, a champagne flute half raised. Her mother sat beside him, her face a shade of red Oz had never seen before. Elliot looked like he was ready to jump up and applaud. The bride and groom were...stunned, for lack of a better word.

And in the middle of the room, pardoning her way through the sea of seated guests, was Cher. What in the world was she doing?

She looked up and saw him standing there. That sunshine smile of hers spread across her face, her eyes shining with such a radiant glow his heart nearly stopped at the sheer beauty of her. That smile was for him. Because of *him*. And suddenly he knew, *knew*, that he'd just found his future.

She pulled up the hem of her dress and pushed her way through the crowded seats. He barreled toward her, meeting her halfway. She opened her arms and he wrapped his around her waist, sweeping her off her feet. Their lips met and he kissed her for all he was worth. Her hands clutched at him like she couldn't believe he was really there. She pulled away, laughing, then kissed him again.

Oz put Cher back on her feet but kept his arms firmly

around her. He stroked a hand down her cheek.

"I didn't get the job."

She pulled away so she could look full into his face. "I don't care."

The hope smoldering in his chest burned a little brighter. He smiled down at her. "You don't?"

"Not in the slightest. I just want you to be happy."

"*Hmm*," he said, running a thumb along her bottom lip. "I can think of a few things that might accomplish that."

She rubbed against him. "*Hmm*, I'm sure you can." She leaned in like she wanted to tell him a secret. "I applied for the MBA program at UNC Chapel Hill. That's near you, isn't it?"

His heart was a burning blaze now. "You did what?"

She shrugged, a sly smile on her lips. "I'm going to get my business degree and open my own center for disadvantaged women."

What the hell was she talking about? "Center for disadvantaged women, what?"

"Yes, like I told you about. An expansion on what DressHer does."

DressHer? He'd heard of that place. It helped women who were reentering the workforce. A lot of them were either single moms, or women leaving abusive relationships. Some ladies just needed to find something better but hadn't had the chance before. DressHer helped them with appropriate clothing, setting up job interviews, all kinds of things. Suddenly, all the comments Cher had made about her job made sense. "*That's* where you work?"

"Yes."

He wrapped his arms around her even tighter. "Personal

shopper, my ass."

He felt her shrug but didn't let go.

"It's sort of a personal shopper."

He leaned down and kissed the tip of her nose. "What does your family think?"

"To hell with my family. I'm finally going after what *I* want. And Oz…I want you."

Before he could question her again, she rose on her toes and pressed her lips to his. His hands cupped her face and he poured every ounce of joy coursing through him into his kiss.

To his surprise, a few of the guests around them started to clap. Cher looked around and laughed. Eventually the whole tent's inhabitants, minus her parents, of course, were cheering. Elliot whooped loudly from his spot back at the family's table.

"Let's get out of here," she said.

"You sure about that?"

She gazed right into his eyes. "More sure than I've ever been about anything in my life." She took his hand. "What do you say, Oz? Will you date me?"

He laughed and scooped her into his arms. "It would be my pleasure Ms. Debusshere."

Epilogue

O z's deep belly-laugh rang out again and Cher smiled. Really, the man could start a party no matter where they were. She moved forward a few feet, her anxiety kicking up a few notches. They were late. Again. But at least they were finally within a few feet of the security check point. Cher checked her watch.

"We're going to miss our flight."

Oz excused himself from the conversation he was having with an older gentleman behind them and came to stand beside her. He checked his own watch.

"Ah. We'll make it. Your watch is fast."

"It is not."

"Yes it is. You always set it ten minutes ahead so we aren't late."

She huffed, but the smile tugging at her lips sort of ruined the effect. "Well, that didn't work today, did it?"

"No. But that wasn't my fault. You set the alarm for the

wrong time."

She opened her mouth to argue but shut it again with a grumble. She hated it when he was right. "I had the time right. I just had the a.m./p.m. setting wrong. Could happen to anyone."

"Sure. But it happens to you at least twice a week. If you didn't own your own shop you would have been fired by now."

"Oh shut up. It's easy for you to say. You get to work from home on your articles all day. I'm the one that has to actually leave the house."

"Very true." Oz wrapped an arm around her waist, pulling her against him for a thorough kiss.

"Congratulations!" The man Oz had been talking with waved at them as he was called over to a second security line that had just opened.

Cher sighed. "Why couldn't they have moved us over?"

"Oh stop being so pissy. We're almost to the front now."

"I'm not being pissy. We're going to miss our flight."

"I didn't realize I was marrying such a grouch."

Cher rolled her eyes, though she couldn't keep a small smile from her lips. "You just hush. And take off your shoes. We're next."

Oz grinned and took off his flip flops, tossing them into the first empty bin. "You know you love me."

"Yeah, yeah. Move the line along, Oserkowski. We've got fifteen minutes to make our flight or we're going to be late for our own wedding."

They emptied their pockets and Cher put her bag on the conveyor belt. This time she'd made sure there were no unapproved items in it. She was taking no chances of getting stopped again.

Oz went through the metal detectors and started gathering their things on the other side. Cher took a deep breath and went through.

The machine *beeped*.

"What! But I'm not wearing anything metal. I even took my engagement ring off."

"Please step this way, ma'am."

"Oh, no. Not again."

"Ma'am, this way."

Cher looked to Oz for help but he was nearly prostrate with laughter.

She glowered at him and went through the second screening. When the security guard wanded her, Cher nodded over at Oz. "We're on our way to our wedding."

The guard laughed and turned to Oz. "Sorry. I'll return her in just a moment."

Oz just gave the guy a thumbs-up and stood back to watch. Traitor.

The guard waved the stupid wand thingy over Cher. It went off when it waved across her shirt.

"All the sequins must be setting it off. Are they metal backed?"

Cher looked down at the Here Comes the Bride shirt that Tyler had made for her. He'd bedazzled it himself. Oz's matching Groom shirt was done in puffy paint. No metal-backed sequins for him.

"I guess so," she said, shaking her head. What were the chances?

By the time they finally got cleared, they were down to five minutes.

"Come on, Debusshere, let's haul ass!" Oz said, grabbing her hand to drag her along after him.

"These legs only go so fast, Oserkowski!" she said, panting in an effort to keep up with him.

They made it to the gate just as the doors were closing.

"Wait!" they shouted.

The attendant looked at the woman behind the counter. She glanced at their shirts, her expression softening.

"All right. The doors aren't technically closed, yet. Let them through."

Cher breathed a sigh of relief as they hurried through the doors and onto the plane. They slipped into their seats, looked at each other, and smiled.

Oz leaned over and kissed her, his hand cupping her cheek. "You have the absolute worst luck."

Cher smiled at him, her heart overflowing with happiness. "Oh, I don't know. I was pretty lucky the day I met you."

"Now *that* I won't argue. Of course, that was almost two years ago. Your luck might be wearing off."

"Not a chance." She threaded her fingers through his. "I love you, Nathaniel."

"Oz."

"Ox."

"Nag."

"Husband?"

Oz grinned. "Now that one I like. Wife."

Cher laughed and leaned over to kiss him.

"You're perfect," he whispered to her.

"No," she said back. "Just perfectly happy."

Acknowledgments

To Erin Molta, my amazing editor — you are always awesome but with this one you have truly outdone yourself. Flat out tremendous. I really don't know what I'd do without you. Thank you so much for everything. You go above and beyond, always. And to Heather Howland — this book literally would not exist without you and I can't tell you how honored I am to be a part of its creation. I can't wait to work on more with you! Thank you so much for your amazing ideas and insights and for all the incredible work you put into these stories.

To Sarah Ballance–you are not only my writing twin but have become one of my truest friends. My days just aren't complete without our minimum 100 emails (it's probably scary that that's not an exaggeration!). They definitely make deadlines easier to cope with. Thank you for always being there, for making me laugh, for pushing me to do better, for having confidence in me when I don't have it in myself, and for *getting* me, quirks and all.

To my writing peeps and amazing support crew—don't know how I'd do it without you. Thank you so much for all your support!

And of course to my amazing husband and kids. Hon, I can't thank you enough for everything you do to make my dream possible. Love you more than I can say. And my sweet kids, thanks for putting up with your crazy, distracted mom. You are my everything.

About the Author

Kira Archer resides in Pennsylvania with her husband, two kiddos, and far too many animals in the house. She tends to laugh at inappropriate moments, break all the rules she gives her kids (but only when they aren't looking), and would rather be reading a book than doing almost anything else. She has odd, eclectic tastes in just about everything and often lets her imagination run away with her. She loves a vast variety of genres and writes in quite a few. If you love historical romances, check out her alter ego, Michelle McLean.